ROGUE RAMRODS

ROGUE RAMRODS

by

Hal Jons

The Golden West Large Print Books
Long Preston, North Yorkshire,
BD23 4ND, England.

First published in Great Britain by Frederick Muller Ltd.

Copyright © MCMLXV Hal Jons

Cover illustration © Marcus Garrett by arrangement with Arcangel Images

A catalogue record for this book is available from the British Library

Published in Large Print 2013 by arrangement with Hal Jons, care of Mrs M Kneller

The Golden West Large Print is an imprint of Library Magna Books Ltd.

Printed and bound in Great Britain by
T.J. (International) Ltd., Cornwall, PL28 8RW

CHAPTER ONE

The sourdough busy tethering his flea-bitten saddle horse and burro to the hitchrail outside the Casino saloon looked no different from a thousand other sourdoughs who had come and gone. He could have been anything from thirty to eighty. A thick stubble of black beard covered his face and his clothes were so stiff with dirt they would have stood up by themselves. The few men moving around the sidewalk of Twin Springs did not spare the man a glance. Pretty soon though they would be mighty interested in him.

He stomped up the three steps to the sidewalk and shuffled his way into the Casino. It was fairly crowded but he elbowed his way to the bar.

The bartender glanced along the bar, taking in the sourdough, and slid his eyes back to the more prosperous-looking customers. He served a couple of drinks to some punchers who had just come in and still ignored the prospector.

'Hey you!' the man's voice reverberated around the saloon. 'Get me a bottle – and fast!'

The bartender moved slowly up the bar. He was a big man and always eager for a chance to show his strength. He considered the sourdough fair game.

'And it's a bottle of what you're wanting?' he asked in a bantering sort of tone.

The years seemed to drop from the prospector and the eyes that fastened on the bartender were bleak.

'Bourbon,' he snarled.

Joe Mears ignored the inference of the man's gaze and leaned over the bar.

'You show me the colour of your money an' you get bourbon. If you're broke like most of your breed I'll throw you out on your neck.'

He was too slow to dodge the pile-driver right hand that exploded in his face and he slid slowly out of sight behind the bar.

The surprised customers surged and took a closer look at the sourdough who was busily delving through his numerous coats for money. Steve Daniels, the owner of the Casino, came out from his office and looked doubtfully from his prone employee to the unkempt prospector. His eyes stood out as though on stalks as the man's hand came away with a bulging money sack. There was a hush in the saloon as the man untied the leather neck thongs and shook out a couple of nuggets on the counter. Heads craned forward to get a closer look and Daniels bellied up close, respect in his eyes.

'You said bourbon, Mister?' he said, reaching under the bar. 'I reckon you'll find this to your taste.'

The prospector nodded and shook out a few more huge nuggets. Then with a grin he swept all but one back into the sack, which he returned to his pocket.

'Guess that'll cover the bourbon and drinks for everyone,' he said as he drew out the cork from his bottle. His eyes glittered a little with grim humour as Daniels' hand closed greedily over the nugget.

The occupants of the saloon were now crowded into a tight bunch around the sourdough. Joe Mears hauled himself up and looked stupidly at the nugget Daniels was weighing carefully in his hand. The prospector tipped up the bottle and drank his way through half a pint of bourbon before lowering it. He wiped his mouth with the back of his sleeve and belched noisily. Slowly he drained the rest of the liquid and nodded for another.

Daniels opened one for him and all eyes watched the man make inroads into the second bottle. Many minds held the same thought; it should be mighty easy to prise the money sack from the old coot if he kept up this rate of drinking. The prospector's next words dispelled these thoughts.

'Any Land Office in this hyar town?' he asked.

Daniels shook his head slowly. 'Nope. The nearest is in Rawlins an' that's twenty-five miles south.'

The sourdough nodded and elbowed his way down the bar apiece. He ignored the pressing throng and took another long pull at his bottle. Daniels followed him after a while, an avaricious gleam in his eyes.

'You set on filing a claim, old-timer?' he asked.

It was a long time before the man answered. He looked around the pressing ring of faces as though weighing up just how much to tell.

'Well, I reckon I might as well tell you folks,' he said at length. 'The news'll break anyway as soon as I hit Rawlins, and my pard's sitting right on our stake.'

The ring around him tightened as he drew breath.

'It's just the biggest lode ever,' he continued. 'For about five miles the gold's showing under the rim of the rock. It sure explains why placer gold's been panned in the valley. Look's like the lode runs clear through the mountain.'

'What mountain?' Daniels couldn't wait for the man's rambling to get to the point.

'Seminoe Peak, that's the one forty miles north-west, dead in line with the Essex and Wind River Peak.'

'Seminoe Peak!' The name was echoed by

most of the men crowding the prospector.

'That mountain's been near turned over since old Jed Angers hit town with a saddle-roll full of fool's gold.' Daniels took a closer look at the nugget he held while he spoke, but he knew gold when he saw it.

'Well, no one travelled up the creek where the Little Caspar runs down to join the North Platte.' The prospector took another pull at his bottle then set it down as though he'd finished with it. 'Halfway up that creek, on the left, the Little Caspar is joined by another stream. Two miles up alongside that stream, about twenty feet above water level, the gold shows, an' it runs true in a thin lode for five miles. I guess there's plenty for everyone.'

Everybody had heard the man's words. They all knew the place he mentioned and there was no need for him to repeat himself. There was a long silence then men started to move. One after another they left the saloon, bent upon rustling up provisions and high-tailing it fast to Seminoe Peak. A few minutes later only the sourdough, Daniels and the bartender Mears remained.

'You look after things Joe,' Daniels said at length. 'I'll go stake us a claim.'

Joe Mears' disbelieving gaze followed his boss as Daniels hurried out through the bat-wing doors. He switched his gaze to the prospector.

11

'Guess I can overlook that sledge-hammer you threw at me, old timer,' he said. 'Considering you've put me in the way of a fortune.' He placed another bottle of bourbon on the counter. 'On the house,' he added. 'No call for me to hang around. Ain't gonna be any customers for quite some time.'

The prospector nodded and his eyes glittered as the bartender followed in the wake of his boss. Collecting the bottle the man moved over to a table and sat down. As he listened to the rising tempo of activity in Twin Springs an air of satisfaction seemed to settle on him.

The news was out with a vengeance now. Riders with hastily-packed saddle rolls were streaming out of town. Men were yelling instructions and throwing provisions down to pardners stocking up wagons of all shapes and sizes. Traders were shuttering up their premises and joining in the rush. Every saddle-horse and every wagon carried their quota of picks and shovels. Dust rose in an ever increasing cloud as the exodus got under way and at last, no more than half an hour after he had told his story of gold in Seminoe Peak, the prospector was left in what seemed sole possession of Twin Springs.

At length he pushed his chair away and walking round the bar collected a couple of bottles, which he stowed away in the depths of one of his many coats. Then with an easy gait, so different from the shambling shuffle he had used on entry to Twin Springs, he went out to his horse and burro. Untethering them from the hitchrail and tying the burro's lead rein to the saddle cantle of his horse, he stepped up into the saddle and headed south towards Rawlins. He grinned as he passed the bank and saw the figures of two men inside. He reckoned he'd cut the town down to size.

A few miles out on the Rawlins trail he branched off into a defile leading out of a deep canyon and headed his mount up the narrow twisting grade. The defile opened out and flattened off, and way in front a man stood between two big boulders awaiting the prospector's approach.

'Hiya, Dave,' he said as the prospector's stringy mount came to a halt. 'The gold fever struck 'em yet?'

'Sure thing, Slim. Only time I ever saw a town clear so fast was when the plague hit Ogalla a few years back.'

Slim grinned and stood aside to let Dave ride past the boulders and on into a small grass-covered valley. Halfway along the valley, under a huge overhang of rock, a ring of men sat around a fire, yarning and smoking. As Dave rode up most of them stood and greeted him. He climbed down from his horse and held out his hand for the mug of coffee one of the men offered.

13

'Well, how did it go?'

The speaker was a tall, well-knit man, with dark handsome features and eyes so grey that they were almost opaque. He looked as he was: the undisputed leader.

'Ain't no more than two men left in Twin Springs, Lew. It's my guess one of those'll be headin' for the gold strike afore sundown.'

There was nothing of the slow-moving sourdough about Dave Cawson now. His face was animated and tough. Animal vitality showed through his every movement.

'I reckon the banker'll stay put. He'll figure he'll make plenty out of a gold strike by sittin' on his fan.'

There was a general round of laughter at Dave's words and a smile flitted over Lew Dillon's severe features.

'I reckon we'll do Rushland a favour salivating him before the news breaks that there just isn't any gold strike. You'd better grab some shut-eye Dave. We'll head for Twin Springs at sundown.'

The two riders looked around curiously as they rode into Twin Springs. Nothing stirred, nobody and nothing evinced any interest in them.

'Something strikes me mighty funny about this hyar town, Clint.'

The speaker was the handsome dapper

Mexican astride the big pinto. His companion, of stocky build, with thick black curly hair crowding down on to his forehead, nodded.

'Yeah, it's got the smell of emptiness an' yet the place is nearly all fresh painted.' He shrugged his broad shoulders. 'Well, I guess all ghost towns looked the same way some time.' Clint Bellamy scraped at the clogging dust in his throat before adding: 'I sure hope someone's left to rustle up enough drink to clear all the alkali we've swallowed.'

The two pardners drew their mounts to a halt outside the most garish saloon bearing the sign Casino and after casting cautious glances up and down the deserted Main Street they tethered their horses to the hitchrail and mounted the sidewalk, pushing their way through the batwing doors into the saloon. A couple of pack rats scuttled across the room to safety, leaving the two men in sole possession.

'Looks like there was plenty of life here just a couple days ago,' remarked Mex, drawing his finger across one of the tables, marking out a trail in the dust.

'Yeah.' Clint Bellamy nodded. 'An' they left in such an almighty hurry they didn't finish their drinks.' He walked around the back of the long bar, and pulling down a bottle of rye from one of the shelves filled a couple of clean glasses. 'What do you suppose got into

15

all those hombres to light out together?' he asked after tossing the contents of one of the glasses down his throat.

'That's what I've been trying to figure.'

Mex sauntered round the bar to join Clint as he spoke. His eyes lit up as he saw a box of Gaucho cheroots behind a row of bottles. Clint groaned as Mex took the box and threw some currency in its place. Grinning at his pard's discomfiture Mex proceeded to light one up.

'Only two things would empty a town this way, Clint,' he continued when he had his cheroot burning nicely. 'An' that's the plague or some galoot in the next town giving a fortune away to the first feller to greet him.'

'Or mebbe three things. If enough hombres smoked those blamed cheroots that'd clear most folk.'

Clint moved up to the bar, taking his re-filled glass with him. Mex was unabashed and drew on his cheroot with keen enjoyment.

'I'm plum curious anyway,' he said. 'Let's take a look-see around town before we push on to Rawlins.'

They drank enough to slake the alkali then left the saloon to make the rounds of the town. Starting on one side they pushed open each door. Everywhere they found the same signs of hasty departure, the pattern becoming almost monotonous until they

16

came to the bank.

The legend proclaimed it as Rushlands Bank. They reckoned that Rushland was one of the two cadavers lying in the middle of the room amidst the dark stains that could only have been caused by blood.

Together Clint and Mex examined the two dead men. There was no doubt they had been dead for at least a day. Just one bullet had been enough in each case.

The pards looked at each other significantly and turned their attention to a search of the bank. A trap door hidden under the carpet led to the dug-out underground room that housed the big safe. The heavy safe door was open. Whoever had salivated the corpses up above had made a fair job of liquidating the bank's assets.

'Well, one thing's for sure. Someone stayed on to do this.' Clint took a look inside the safe as he spoke and shrugged his wide shoulders. 'I guess this rules out the plague having emptied the town.'

Mex nodded and made his way back up the wooden stairway to the office floor. Clint followed thoughtfully.

'Y'know Clint, it's my guess the smart thing for us to do is hightail for Rawlins pronto.' The Mexican's face was unusually serious. 'Mighty soon folk are going to come back into town an' they'll be asking questions. If they don't get the right answers

17

maybe they'll get to jumping to the wrong conclusions.'

'That makes good sense to me, Mex,' Bellamy replied. 'But somehow I've a feeling I couldn't drag you as far as Rawlins unless you knew just what had emptied this town.'

'I'll admit I'm curious,' Mex grinned, his white teeth gleaming. 'But I don't aim to be around to answer questions.' He started out of the office. 'There's nothing we can do for these hombres. Let's hit the trail.'

Mex was at the door when he turned around and shot a warning glance at Clint, but the stocky Texan had already heard the sounds of a rapidly approaching stage-coach.

'Better get the answers ready,' he grunted. 'We've got company.'

They emerged from the bank and stood leaning against the sidewalk rail as the six-team stage-coach rolled past and ground to a stop outside the staging depot. They stayed where they were while the driver climbed down and opened up the passenger door. Three people alighted on to the dusty road but only one took the eye of the pards.

The girl was tall, lissom and breath-takingly beautiful, dressed in pale blue and wearing a wide straw hat with ash blonde curls peeping under the brim. She brought some pleasantly cool relief to the sun scorched scene.

Unwillingly Clint and Mex took stock of the two men who had been the girl's co-passengers. One, a burly hard-looking man, toted a badge. The other, tall, dark, of striking appearance, handed the girl up the steps to the sidewalk and walked beside her towards the pardners. The driver, wiry and sprouting whiskers all over his face, got busy hauling down the baggage. The Marshal stood gazing up and down the length of Main Street, scratching his head in a bewildered manner until his gaze fastened on the pardners, when he started heading towards them.

The girl and her companion were almost abreast of the pardners when it became apparent that they were about to turn into the bank. Mex, being nearest, stepped back from the rail and placed his arm out, barring their path. The girl flashed him a surprised look from eyes big and blue but the man beside her fastened two cold implacable eyes upon the urbane smiling Mexican.

'I wouldn't go in there, Ma'am,' Mex said quietly. 'Some hombre's been there already with a gun.'

A look of alarm crossed the girl's face. She broke away from her companion and pushing past Mex, rushed inside the bank. The man followed her at a slower speed.

'Where in heck's everybody? An' who in

blazes are you?' The lawman stood glaring up at the two men as though he held them responsible for the empty street and departed townsfolk.

Before either man could answer the girl's scream rang out and the Marshal rushed up the steps. He stopped at the bank doorway and peered inside, then seeing the girl kneeling beside one of the prone figures he added up the score and turned to face the pardners. He was no slouch with a gun and in an easy flowing movement he confronted the pards with an unwavering long-handled Colt.

'Just unbuckle those gunbelts and let 'em fall. One fast move an' I'll salivate the pair of you.'

Neither Clint nor Mex moved to do his bidding. Mex gave the man a pitying look.

'You're sure jumping to conclusions,' he said. 'You see a coupla dead men and straight away reckon the fellers nearest 'em are the killers. Your sort of lawman sure gets me jumpy.'

The Colt stayed pointing in their general direction and the Marshal looked just as firmly convinced of their guilt. He was about to repeat his instruction when Clint broke in.

'If you'd care to have a look at those broncs of ours you'll see we just rode in, then check on the corpses and you'll find they've been dead quite some time. When we rode in we got plumb curious why there were no folk around and took a look around town. We'd just found the dead men before you arrived.'

While Clint was talking the girl returned to the sidewalk, the man's protective arm around her. There was a sneering expression on his face as he took in the situation.

'Don't let 'em smooth talk you, Jess,' he said to the Marshal. 'I guess they did the killing an' it's my bet they've emptied the safe and stashed it all away somewhere then ridden back in so that they could put an innocent front on things.'

'Now that's real unfriendly, Mister,' said Mex easily, 'I can't say I like hombres who jump to conclusions too fast.'

'Cut the talking and let those gunbelts drop,' snarled the Marshal. 'I'll sort you out when I've got you in the pokey.'

There was a mean look about him when he spoke and the pards did as they were told.

'You're mebbe right about 'em, Lew,' the Marshal growled as the gunbelts clattered to the sidewalk. 'I'm sure sorry about your pa, Miss Kathy. I'll see to it these coyotes get stretched for it.'

Clint and Mex exchanged significant glances. The situation could become tricky. The teamster who had followed in the Marshal's wake and taken a look inside the bank didn't help any.

21

'Get 'em strung up, Jess,' he cackled. 'That's the way to deal with bank robbers. What d'you say, Mister Dillon?'

'Huh, we ain't checked that they've robbed the bank yet Rube,' Lew Dillon replied. 'But I'll lay a dime to a dollar the safe's empty. I guess we can leave the neck-tie party until the folk get back to town.'

'Yeah, where in heck's everybody?' Rube asked, his whiskers quivering.

'That's something these hombres might be able to tell us.' Dillon spat the words out then turned to the girl who was composing herself after the shock of finding her father dead. 'Come along, Miss Kathy,' he said. 'I'll see you home. You can leave things here to me.'

'Th-thank you, Mister Dillon,' she managed then after a doubtful glance at the pards, she turned and allowed herself to be led away by the tall, good-looking Dillon.

'Get goin' you hombres,' the Marshal grated. 'Bring along the hardware, Rube.'

Clint and Mex turned and walked in front of the lawman and teamster until they came to the gaol-house. The Marshal kicked the door open and prodded them inside. Rube followed and hung the gunbelts on a couple of nails.

'Let's have your monickers,' the Marshal said as he lifted down a key-ring from its hook.

'The name's Bellamy, Clint Bellamy.' The Texan's eyes bored into the Marshal as he spoke.

'And Cristobal di Stephano Juarez,' Mex put in with a light grin. 'What's yours?'

As the Marshal stared back at him Mex calmly searched for and found a cheroot. He lit it and blew smoke derisively in the lawman's direction. Clint eyed his pard for his cue to move. He could tell that Mex was itching to turn the tables on the stiff-necked Marshal.

'Jarman is the name, greaser. Marshal of this hyar burg.' He nodded towards the open door leading to the cells. 'Get going, the pair of you.'

Rube the teamster looked on with approval in his bird-sharp eyes and the pards headed through the door followed by the Marshal. Clint caught Mex's warning glance and waited meekly outside a cell as Jarman opened a door. When the pards filed in he replaced his gun in his holster and slammed the door. He was about to turn the key when the Mexican's cool voice made him look up. The little Derringer that pointed at his stomach appeared as big as a cannon and the eyes of the suave Mexican were as cold as the tomb.

'Now open up again you lobo-brained maverick or I'll drill you sure as hell.'

The Marshal backed away in alarm. Mex

23

pushed the grilled cell door open and went through. Clint followed rapidly, then moving round his pardner relieved Jarman of his guns. Rube the teamster came to the door leading to the gaol office at that moment. He gobbled a bit at the change in circumstances but froze when Clint covered him.

'You won't get away feller,' Jarman snarled as he backed away. He stopped short as Mex's finger tightened a little on the trigger. When the Mexican motioned him towards the office he went slowly ahead into the room. Rube had already edged up against the table under the menace of Jarman's guns held by the able-looking Bellamy.

'All you small-town marshals are the same,' Mex said, his eyes glinting evilly. 'Ain't got the common sense of a half-grown steer an' ready to grasp at the nearest stranger as responsible for anything from rustling to murder.'

Jarman said nothing. He was just swearing inwardly for not having searched his prisoners thoroughly for hidden weapons.

'We may or may not leave the territory, Jarman,' Mex added. 'But if we're of a mind to get away you won't stop us. I reckon you'd do better to contact Sheriff Myers at Rawlins. He knows me well enough to give a clean bill of health. That might save you wasting time and effort.'

Jarman's lips curled. 'Huh, you're mighty

safe gettin' Myers to vouch for you. He got dry-gulched a few weeks back.'

A pained look fleeted across the Mexican's face then he shot a quick glance at Clint.

'I'll look after these hombres if you'll get the broncs. I reckon Jarman's too stiff-necked to look further than his nose so we might as well get clear away.'

Clint nodded and before going out into the street he retrieved their gunbelts, fixing his own into place and slinging his pard's over his shoulder. When he got down from the sidewalk he saw the man Dillon making his way from the other end of town. Without haste he continued to where his big dun gelding and the Mexican's pinto stood in full equine dignity and patience. He had one eye on Dillon as he untethered the animals and took his time giving Dillon a chance to get alongside.

'Looks like you persuaded Jarman that you didn't do the killin',' Dillon remarked as he stopped and looked down from the sidewalk.

'What's it to you?' Clint snapped. 'I guess what passed between the marshal and us ain't none of your business.'

The man's grey eyes narrowed and his face looked as though carved in stone.

'Everything's my business in Twin Springs, Mister.' His voice was flat, expressionless, and Clint saw him loosen into the gunman's pose.

'Howso?' he asked.

'The Dillons made this town, Mister, an' it's Dillon money that's kept it goin', that's why.'

Clint shrugged and half turned away.

'That still doesn't make you the law, an' you still cut no ice with me Dillon.'

For an instant it looked as though Dillon was going for his gun and Clint made a one-hand draw with rapier-like speed. Dillon's eyes mocked him as the man relaxed into an easy pose.

'I guess you'd say you were mighty fast with the shooting irons,' he said easily. 'Could be that you ain't fast enough after all if I had a mind to accommodate you. Maybe I'll do just that if I get to provin' you did rob the bank an' salivate Dan Rushland and Cressy.'

'Yeah, that's as maybe,' growled the Texan. 'But for now unhitch that gunbelt and let it drop.' Dillon tensed again but moved to comply as Clint continued: 'Make it real slow an' you'll go on breathing. I wouldn't worry too much if I had to salivate you to get clear of Twin Springs.'

The gunbelt dropped to the sidewalk and on instructions from Clint, Dillon kicked it down into the roadway. Cautiously Clint bent down and picked it up. He took the lead rein of the two horses and motioned Dillon to walk along the sidewalk. When they reached the gaol Mex prodded the marshal and teamster outside to join Dillon, who eyed the proceedings with interest.

'So that's the way of it, eh?' he said. 'You couldn't square yourselves with alibis an' you're getting out.' He shrugged. 'Well, just see how far you get. You'll still dangle on a rope right here in Main Street.'

'Maybe Mister,' put in Mex, his teeth gleaming as he smiled. 'But don't reckon on enjoying the spectacle. I promise to have you bedded down in Boot Hill before that unlikely event.'

The Mexican dropped down to the road-way as he spoke and took his mount's lead rein from Clint. Before they could get into the saddle they heard the hoofbeats thud down Main Street. A rider approached quickly and they saw the gleam of hope spring into the eyes of their captives. Another expression flitted across Dillon's face. It contained hatred and countless other ingredients.

CHAPTER TWO

The rider took in the situation quickly enough. He slowed his horse twenty yards or so away from the group to keep with the initiative.

'Keep coming, feller,' Clint called out. 'An' keep your hands away from the hardware.'

The rider hauled his mount to a stop just where he was.

'Reckon I can take my chance from here,' he volunteered.

Clint nodded. 'Yeah, but if you do, I'll salivate Lew Dillon an' considering he's top man hereabouts, that should cause you some concern.'

The laugh that escaped the newcomer was genuine and infectious.

'Considering Lew Dillon holds a note on my spread that's gonna take my every last nickel today, I might do myself a service going for the hardware.'

There was something fresh and clear cut about the newcomer that appealed to both Clint and Mex, and they gave him further appraisal without relaxing their attention on the other three men. He was no more than twenty-three, of medium height and slender build, dark-haired with lazy blue eyes. His face was set in good humoured lines but the set of his chin gave the close observer the clue that he would never be hustled or forced to back down.

'What's the play anyway?' the youngster added. 'And where in tarnation is everybody? You fellers cleared the town with those six-guns of yours?'

'Nope.' Mex shook his head emphatically. 'Some hombres shot up a coupla fellers in the bank an' robbed it, an' the marshal an' Dillon seem to favour us as the guilty parties.'

A look of concern flooded the newcomer's features and he dismounted slowly. Ignoring any possible danger from Clint and Mex he hurried to the bank. They let him go but curiosity held them until minutes later he emerged. His face had paled under his tan when he came back to them. He said nothing for a long time, during which he studied the pardners intently. Significantly he hooked his thumbs in front of his gunbelt and he turned his attention to Dillon.

'Looks like that note will have to lay over until we find the jaspers who did the bank steal, Dillon,' he said in a quiet voice.

Dillon shook his head and his face was set hard.

'Oh no, Matt. I guess I've lost a durned sight more money outa that safe than you but it won't affect my business. Any debts

30

I've got, I'll honour, an' you can do the same. If you don't pay out on that note by sun-up tomorrow I'm taking over the Triple Bar.' He paused and nodded towards the pardners. 'Mebbe if you don't lose sight of these hombres you'll still get the money back to square the debt.'

'I reckon that's good sense, Nugent,' put in Marshal Jarman but without any enthusiasm. Clint and Mex held all the aces for the present and it was apparent that Matt Nugent wouldn't turn the tables.

Nugent ignored the marshal. His gaze was fixed on Lew Dillon.

'Maybe you'll have another think before trying to take over the Triple Bar, Dillon,' he growled. 'Or else there's gonna be some grief on this range.'

Dillon's face darkened and it was obvious that the guns held by the pardners irked him.

'The grief will be all yours Nugent if you try to stop me. If you can't pay off the note before sun-up the Triple Bar is legally mine an' the law's gonna back my play. That so, Jarman?' he asked turning to the marshal.

Jarman nodded.

Matt Nugent turned abruptly. Ignoring the pards he stepped up into the saddle and gigged his mount, a wall-eyed black mare, into a canter, heading south. With the little scene played out Clint and Mex had no call to stay, and swinging into their saddles they rode out of town on the heels of Nugent's spirited mare.

A couple of miles out of town Nugent realized he was being followed and drew rein, then turned around to face the oncoming riders. He made no move for his guns as they came up.

'You fellers going some place?' he asked quietly.

They nodded. 'Yeah, Twin Springs seems a mite unfriendly. We thought maybe Rawlins'll be more hospitable.' Clint's homely face split into a grin as he spoke and Nugent weighed his words before replying.

'If you did the killing back in town you'll find Rawlins inhospitable pretty soon. The news'll break just as soon as the stage makes the return run, and in any case Jarman'll be raising a posse to trail you.'

'It's going to be tough work rustling up a posse in Twin Springs,' Mex put in as he lit a cheroot. 'But we'll worry about that when they catch up with us.'

'You came into town from the north,' Clint remarked. 'Howcome you're headed south now?'

Nugent hauled his horse around and set off at any easy pace. He waved the pardners alongside and they rode along in silence for a while before he answered Clint's question.

'I'm heading for Rawlins to see a couple friends in the hope of raising enough to meet the note Dillon holds. But I'm not too optimistic.'

'Howcome he holds your note?' Mex asked conversationally.

Nugent glared at him. Like most cattle men he resented any intrusion into his private affairs, but the Mexican's disarming smile took away the edge of his temper. As they rode along he scrutinized the two men closely, arriving at the same conclusion he had formed of them in Twin Springs. They were men to ride the river with. His reserve ebbed away as he thought back over the events that led to his present predicament and in a way he welcomed the chance of talking to get things into perspective.

'Luke Dillon and my father hit the terri-tory together,' he said. 'They'd been pards for a long time and reckoned it'd be a good idea to run spreads alongside each other. Well they both prospered an' got married to a couple of gals who stayed in Twin Springs a few weeks with a wagon train heading for Oregon.' He paused a while and rolled himself a cigarette before continuing.

'Dillon was a thruster but my father was mighty tough too. Being neighbours sort of lost its savour as the years passed and only the friendship of my mother and Dillon's wife stopped the two men falling out. But even so they tried to outsmart each other in cattle deals. Anyway my mother died and shortly after Dillon's wife got killed by a rogue horse. The Dillons and Nugents got out of the habit of visiting and became just two big spreads pushing hard.'

The picture was clear enough to the pards and they were both now intensely interested.

'Then my father got around to thinking he'd like me to be something more than just a cattleman and I went east to college. He made out that I'd do better to stay east until I'd finished my schooling so I stayed on for three years. What I didn't know though was that my father's health changed rapidly, until a few months before I'd finished my course I heard he was dead. His last instruction was that I'd stay on to finish what I'd started. When at last I came back to the Triple Bar someone had been stealing us blind. Durkin, our segundo, got dry-gulched along with a couple more tight hands and a few more drifted off.' He pulled hard at his cigarette and exhaled fiercely as he mulled things over.

'Things got worse and when it came to counting heads I couldn't raise enough beef to make the trek to the railhead pay. That's where Lew Dillon came in. We'd been fairly good friends and when he offered to lend me enough to tide over the bad spell and buy in some good breeding stock, I didn't look any further. But Lew's got more of his old man in him than I'd reckoned. Over the last couple of years the friendship's petered out an' I'm willing to swear that he's responsible for the rustling that's gone on. Anyhow I got to grips with things and managed to get a trail herd together. The money I deposited in the bank a coupla days ago ready for settling the account with Dillon.'

'I guess Dillon could wait until the bank makes good your losses,' put in Clint but Nugent shook his head.

'The bank belonged to Rushland, one of the men who were killed. He had no other branches and made most of his money by keeping his interest rate to depositors lower and lending rates higher than the Eastern bank he used. He kept a float of money but the bulk of it was deposited with the Chase National. He was pretty shrewd and his own investments out of profits gave him a comfortable living, but there's no obligation on the part of his next of kin to make good my loss. He was only holding it for me, mainly because I wanted him to witness the payment to Lew Dillon.'

'Who knew the money was there?' asked Mex.

'Rushland and Cressy, but they've got 'emselves killed so they're in the clear. Lew Dillon and his segundo Don Lear because I told Lear to pass on the information to his boss that the money was waiting in the bank to settle the note.'

'Mebbe Lear helped himself, Nugent,' suggested Clint. 'And if he did then it's likely he didn't say anything to Dillon.'

Nugent looked doubtful. 'Nope. Lear is a gunslick an' mighty mean but he's in Dillon's pocket. I don't reckon he'd pull anything like that, not unless he's pulling his freight.'

'That's something to check on,' put in Mex, and Nugent stared at him in surprise; then his expression cleared.

'Huh, I got the impression you were gonna check on that,' he said. 'I guess you mean me?'

'Waal, no, you had it right the first time,' Mex replied slowly. 'We're just naturally curious an' we'd like to know the answers before moving out of the territory.'

Nugent glanced from Mex to Clint, who was smiling his satisfaction.

'What's it to you?' he asked. 'You lawmen?'

'No siree,' Clint said. 'But Mex an' me don't take too well to the high an' mighty attitude of Jarman an' Dillon in trying to fix the murders on us, and moreover we're not struck on the idea of running from Twin Springs so that they're left with the belief they're right.' He shook his head decisively. 'Nope, we'd end up by looking over our shoulders whenever we rode into a town.'

'Another thing,' said Mex. 'We'd like to

36

know why Twin Springs was empty when we rode in.'

Nugent scratched his head then gave that one up. He had too many problems of his own.

'Is the old man Dillon still around?' Clint asked, more to keep the conversation going than for any other reason.

'No, just about a year ago he tripped up and fell down the veranda steps at his spread, the Bar Q. He was carrying a scattergun an' it went off, blowing the best part of his head away.'

'That's a might funny way for a man of his sort to die.' Mex's face expressed surprise as he tried to picture a range-hardened fire-brand meeting his end in such a simple manner, but Nugent added nothing to that.

'Are you gonna be able to stop Dillon taking over the Triple Bar tomorrow?' Clint asked at length.

'I don't know.' The youngster reined his mount in and thought about it. The pardners drew rein and watched the frown gather on his face. 'Nope, I just can't say. If I don't raise the ante in Rawlins I'll have to tell the crew there's no money in the kitty an' we've got a fight on our hands. It's my guess I'll be left with about three men. I don't figure we'll do much good against Dillon.'

Clint and Mex exchanged glances. They liked the way Nugent weighed the situation and intended to place the facts clearly to his crew, and they appreciated his disinclination to accept the possibility that they were killers. Mex nodded imperceptibly.

'We'd sure appreciate being allowed to horn in,' Clint said simply, and the frown on Nugent's face was chased away by surprise.

'You've no call to share in my troubles,' he replied. 'But you're welcome.'

He looked from one to the other and his spirits rose as he took in the Texan's stocky, dependable frame and the lithe, yet lazy-looking Mexican. He reckoned they'd add a core of iron to any cause they backed.

'That being so there's no point in us riding on into Rawlins,' Clint said. 'We'll take a look at your spread.'

Nugent nodded his agreement. 'Ask for Jim Dyer an' tell him you're staying on my sayso.'

'Where does the Triple Bar lie?' asked Mex. 'Maybe there's another way in that misses out Twin Springs?'

'Yeah, there is,' Nugent agreed. 'But it adds about ten miles to the ride. You see those two saw-toothed peaks.' He pointed to the north-west where the mountains just cleared the shimmering heat haze. 'The Triple Bar is due north-east of those peaks, but you'll pick up the trail there running north then east that takes you through the hills that lie north of Twin Springs. The trail picks up with the

Triple Bar where you come to a wide high-walled canyon.'

The pards nodded and with a wave of farewell they turned their mounts off the trail and headed across the rough scrub country towards the saw-toothed hills.

'Here we go sticking our necks out,' grinned Mex as he scanned the terrain with his eagle sharp eyes.

'We heard Jarman says the law would back Dillon in any fight for Nugent's spread. So even if we gets around to catching the killers he'll still have us on his wanted list.'

Clint shrugged his wide shoulders and rolled himself a smoke.

'Y'know Mex,' he said. 'It could be that Dillon's got right on his side an' that for once the big man deserves what he's after, but my instinct tells me the law's backing the wrong horse. For my money Dillon's a lot meaner than Nugent made him out to be!'

'That's the way I figured.' Another thought struck Mex. 'I wonder where that Rushland girl comes into the picture.'

Clint shot a sharp glance at Juarez. He had great respect for the way the Mexican reasoned and his pard's question set his mind ticking back over the last couple of hours.

'Could be she fits right into the middle of things,' he said at length. 'Dillon was mighty attentive, and Nugent stated he didn't expect Rushland's next of kin to make good his losses. I guess he was talking about the girl.'

'She sure is pretty enough to set 'em at each other's throats,' Mex said with conviction. 'Not my style mind,' he added with a smile. 'But pretty enough for most men.'

'Huh, it's more than looks I'll be wanting if I ever get to looking twice at a woman,' Clint said with an air of seriousness.

Mex said nothing but his grin stretched from ear to ear.

They relapsed into companionable silence and the miles slipped away under the easy gait of their mounts. Both men were studying the surrounding country with keen interest. They would be up against men with an intimate knowledge of the terrain and their lives might depend upon memorizing some feature of the country. Mex was lucky in possessing a photographic memory in addition to his natural talent as a scout and tracker, while Clint was keen, observant and careful. Their partnership had matured since the days they had first met on the Randall-Houston spread in Montana, until now, several escapades later, they were bound by an indefinable bond of respect and trust, unspoken but deep. Both men were able gunslingers and when occasion demanded, cold and deadly; altogether a formidable partnership when the chips were down.

They passed between the two saw-toothed

peaks and picked up the trail Nugent had spoken of earlier. For the most part it was rough and strewn with boulders that had dislodged themselves through the years from the bald cliffs that glowered down upon them from both sides. Being in no hurry they allowed their animals to pick their way at their own speed.

After a few miles they reined in where the trail was crossed by another one running to the north west through a series of dry washes. Both men searched their pockets for the smokes they favoured. Clint rolled himself a cigarette and Mex chewed at the end of a cheroot before lighting up. He grinned as Clint moved his big gelding down wind of him. It happened every time until it had become an almost involuntary action on the Texan's part.

'It's my bet this trail leads out of Twin Springs at the south end of a spread the other side of those hills,' Mex said nodding towards a row of foothills to the west. 'One of Nugent's neighbours I guess.'

Clint nodded and they were about to move on when they picked up the sound of hoofbeats.

'Might as well stay an' get ourselves introduced,' he suggested. 'The more folk we know the better.'

The rider was nursing his mount and it was quite some time before he came into

41

sight out of a dry wash.

''Now that's mighty interesting Mex. It's Dillon.' Clint passed a hand over his weather-beaten face and rubbed his chin thoughtfully. 'D'you reckon he'll try his hand at taking us into town on his lonesome?'

There was a glitter in the Mexican's eyes as he shook his head.

'Nope. Not Dillon. His sort don't make a move without the cards are stacked high in his favour.'

Dillon came on, his face impassive. When just a few yards away he hauled his horse to a stop. The light faded from his slate-grey eyes when he looked from one to another, and revealed the innermost depth of the man to be as cold as a mortician's slab.

'You'll have to move a mite faster if you're gonna keep outa Jarman's way,' he said icily.

'Don't go fretting on our account, Dillon,' Clint replied. 'We'll worry about Jarman when we see him, or mebbe Jarman should do the worrying.'

'Tough hombres, eh?' There was a sneer on the man's face that transformed it from dark good looks to ugliness. 'I'll see just how tough you are when you get strung up for the killings back in town.'

'Maybe you'd like to try taking us in?' Mex's voice was silky but Dillon wasn't fooled. He kept his hand conspicuously clear of his guns.

'I can wait,' he growled. 'There's no call for me to do Jarman's job. He'll catch up with you in his own good time.'

Clint shrugged the remark away and he let the easy-going good humour fade from his face.

'You're a windbag, Dillon,' he said. 'And one day your gabbing's gonna give someone itchy fingers. Could be today,' he added nastily.

The hot blood rose up from Dillon's neck until his face was red with anger, but he kept himself in check. Two to one against wasn't his idea of odds for any battle and this one could be a mite too personal. He stared hard at the pards for a full minute, then touching the horse with his spurs he rode off, straight-backed and bristling with anger. Clint and Mex watched him go until he was lost to view. There was a satisfied look on the Mexican's face.

'He looked a bit rattled,' he observed with a grin. 'It sure pays to get a man edgy. He's likely to throw away his best chances by being too impetuous.'

'Yeah, or kill you instead of just throwing a scare into you,' remarked Clint dryly.

Mex merely grinned the wider. 'We may as well break off this trail and cut across Dillon's range to the Triple Bar,' he said. 'We might pick up something of interest.'

'Could be,' the young Texan replied.

'Y'know, I've been wondering whether Dillon just wants his money back or wants to get his hands on Nugent's outfit.'

'It's a point, Clint. I guess we'll know more about that when we've taken a look at the spreads.'

The two men turned their mounts on to the Bar Q trail and followed at a slow speed in Dillon's wake. They rode through the chain of hills and after making their way through an area of rough scree and brush came on to lush range where the grass stood knee high. Turning their mounts towards higher ground they rode on until they were able to command a good view.

Away to the north west the sun glinted on a river that ran out of the far hills. Its course was almost due east and as far as they could judge, ran on into Triple Bar territory. It was good cattle country and Dillon's range was well stocked. Cattle were dotted in varying numbers as far as they could see.

Dillon had never given a backward glance but the pards reckoned he was too wise a bird not to know they were following. They watched him until he was almost lost in the haze and almost indistinguishable from the grazing cattle. Then out of the huddle of animals he merged together with a few dots that separated from the herd, and these moved at speed back along the trail Dillon had taken. Clint nodded towards them.

'I've gotta notion they're set on making things warm for us,' he said. 'That Dillon's mighty keen on getting us strung up so they might be aiming to dispense with the law.'

'We'd better lead them to where we'll hold the aces then,' said Mex and he headed his pinto for the shoulder of the hill.

Clint wheeled his gelding round and followed him. He was content to leave the situation in the capable hands of the Mexican. When they reached the breast of the hill Mex reined in to ensure that the distant riders would see them. When they changed direction he nodded with satisfaction then set his mount down the slope with the breast of the mountain hiding him from the oncoming riders. Clint was close on his heels and smiled grimly as Mex changed course, heading back round the eastern shoulder.

They rode a couple of miles along the rim then downhill back on to the Bar Q Twin Springs trail. Mex knew exactly where he wanted to be and they went through a succession of dry washes and gulches before running through the canyon with towering walls that funnelled at the south end to a width that would barely take a stage coach. A number of large boulders beyond the canyon mouth were in position to control the exit from the canyon of an army, and choosing the most advantageous position Clint and Mex drew rein, slid out the saddle and after removing their rifles took up position.

'Here they come!' announced Mex after they had waited about five minutes.

Clint nodded. He was used to his pard's uncanny knack of picking up sounds seconds before he did. Mex rested his rifle barrel along a flat edge of the boulder and eyed the section of canyon wall that would cause a bullet to richochet with the most noise.

The oncoming riders were pressing their mounts and the sound of hoofbeats thundered through the canyon. Clint shifted his position and checked his guns. The two men exchanged quick glances as the Bar Q men burst into view. Their understanding was complete.

Five riders hurried towards them, the dust rising up in a thick cloud. Mex waited until they were too far from the bend in the canyon to wheel and retrace their steps, then his rifle spoke, one sharp staccato report that reverberated and echoed along the canyon walls. The riders hauled their mounts to a stop, ducking low as the bullet whined and spat from one wall to another.

'Don't move!' yelled Mex. 'Nice an' easy now, slide those gunbelts to the ground.'

The five dust-grimed men stared towards the boulder. The leader, a lithe, hard-faced man, placed his hand deliberately on the saddle pommel.

'What in blazes do you want?' he shouted.

Clint moved out from behind the boulder but the sun glinted on Mex's rifle barrel and the men stayed put.

'That's what we want to know,' Clint said easily. 'You fellers have been sure burning leather on our trail.' The Texan stood four square in front of the horsemen, stocky and grimly purposeful. 'Wa'al, you've caught up with us. What now?' He relapsed into the slow drawl of the Southerner but his soft talk didn't lull the Bar Q men into taking risks.

'I guess you hold the aces hombre,' the leader said calmly. 'So I reckon you'll have a few more hours freedom, but we aimed on taking you into town to get you tried an' strung up.'

'Well, you're not getting much luck.' There was a sneer on Clint's face as he spoke. 'I reckon Dillon's passed on the idea that we robbed the bank an' salivated Rushland and his buddy. Well we didn't an' we don't take kindly to being tagged. If any of you hombres want to be heroes, now's the time.'

There was a long pause when no man moved. The leader eyed the Texan carefully and his men conveyed to him by glances that any action was up to him. He dragged deeply on his courage and Clint saw his adam's apple slide up and down his throat a couple of times. The Texan knew at that moment he had the beating of the man and he made up

47

his mind not to kill.

Just when it appeared the man was not going to fight, he moved at considerable speed. A split second later he was wringing his hand in pain, his gun having been shot out of his hand as soon as it had cleared leather.

'Anybody else?' asked Clint, his smoking gun held nonchalantly at hip level. Nobody moved. 'Well just let those gunbelts drop an' get the Hades back to Dillon.'

Mex emerged from behind the boulder, his rifle aimed at their general direction. The smile on his face was somewhat short of humour and merely highlighted the sinister gleam in his eyes. One by one the men unclasped their gunbelts and let them clatter to the rock floor. The leader picked up the reins and wheeled his horse around. He rode swiftly past the other four men who as quickly followed him. With the thunder of hoofbeats and a cloud of dust the riders rounded the bend without one backward glance.

CHAPTER THREE

'Looks tidy enough,' mused Clint as the two men rode down the grade alongside the corral towards the huddle of ranch buildings. 'Everything newly painted, plenty of good graze too.'

'Yeah, everything bar stock,' put in Mex drily. 'To pay off that note Dillon holds it looks like Nugent scraped nigh on every one last steer.'

They had counted no more than fifty head of cattle from the moment they had run on to Triple Bar range, and although they suspected there would be treble that number dotted around the rest of Nugent's spread, the stock fell far short of a paying proposition for a ranch that size.

A couple of men were busy repairing a section of corral fencing opposite the long low ranch house. They paused and straightened up as the pards rode into the square. One was a stocky, full-faced oldster, the other a spare tired-looking youngster.

'What do you fellers want?' the oldster asked in a gravelly voice.

'Looking for Dyer,' Clint replied.

'That's me. Now what?'

Clint and Mex slid out of their saddles and dusted the alkali out of their clothes.

'Glad to know you, Dyer,' Clint said. 'Nugent told us to tell you he wanted us to stay on here. He's gone into Rawlins and aims to be back before sun-up. My moniker's Bellamy, Clint Bellamy, an' my pard's Mex Juarez.'

Dyer looked at the newcomers doubtfully. 'What does he want in Rawlins?' he asked.

'Enough dinero to stop Dillon taking over this spread tomorrow,' Mex replied. 'The bank in Twin Springs was robbed and a coupla fellers got salivated before Nugent got the money to pay Dillon off. He's got to sun-up to raise the ante. Dillon says he's gonna take over for sure if Nugent can't square the note.'

Dyer and his companion digested the news with grim expressions on their faces.

'An' where do you fit in?' It was the younger man who spoke up.

'We just don't like Dillon,' Clint answered. 'And if Nugent's bent on standing his ground, we reckoned he could do with a bit of help.'

Dyer nodded and turned to the younger man. 'See to their cayuses, Stacey. I'll rustle up some chow for 'em.'

Clint and Mex handed over their lead reins to the young puncher and followed Dyer into the ranch house. The room was big and austerely furnished. It gave the impression that a woman's hand had not touched it for a long time. Dyer motioned them to a couple of chairs and placed a bottle and glasses on the table.

'Help yourselves,' he growled. 'An' if you want to tidy up before eating, the wash house is outside next to the kitchen.'

He turned away and yelled 'Sing! Sing!'

Like magic a weedy-looking Chinaman appeared through the inner doorway and regarded Dyer with a bland expression on his wrinkled face.

'The boss says these fellers Bellamy and Juarez are to stay here. Fix 'em up with some chow, Johnny.'

'Will do, Mister Dyer,' the Chinaman replied. He bowed towards the pards and disappeared as silently as he had arrived.

'How many more hands have you got, Dyer?' Clint asked as he poured out two measures of bourbon.

The foreman rubbed a hand ruefully over his weather-beaten face.

'Eight. I'm expecting 'em back any minute after working the brush on the north range.' He paused and took a bite out of a thick tobacco plug. 'But I wouldn't count on more than three of 'em staying if it comes to a battle. The others are drifters anyway an' only interested in a pay packet.'

'Bit thin to stand out against Dillon then,'

Mex said in between appreciative sips of bourbon.

Dyer shrugged. 'Ain't no use worrying over that. I guess we'd best just wait an' see what happens.' With that he left them.

Clint and Mex eyed each other. The matter wasn't as simple as that. As they saw it the waiting game was all in Dillon's favour. They had a couple more drinks apiece then went to the wash-house to sluice down. When they eventually sat down to eat they were spruced up and free of alkali. The Chinaman hovered around until they cleared every last bit, then left them with steaming mugs of coffee and the pot simmering on the hearth-stove.

'Mighty good chow, Johnny,' Mex said as the man made for the doorway and Clint added his appreciation.

Johnny Sing looked around, a benign smile on his face. 'Glad you liked it. Mebbe if you stay I'll try out some ancestral recipes.'

'Nope, just stick to plain honest chow,' put in Clint hurriedly. 'No birds nest soup for me thank you.'

The cook shrugged his thin shoulders and disappeared into the kitchen.

Mex laughed. 'Reckon you've hurt his feelings Clint.'

'Better his than mine. Birds nest soup don't sound quite civilized to me.'

They smoked and drank coffee in silence

for some time, relaxing in the manner of their kind, but both were mulling over the same problem.

'Beats me, Mex, why Dillon's so keen on getting his money tomorrow,' Clint said at length. 'He's still got time to run another trail herd to the pens before the weather breaks and from what we saw, plenty of stock. It wouldn't hurt him to let the time run on a coupla years.'

'And so you figure he had some hand in making the money disappear outa Rushland's bank? He isn't stuck for dinero but he wants the Triple Bar badly enough to do murder.'

'It could be, Mex, but there could also be some other interested parties, and Dillon might not be the big bad man we've made him out to be.'

'Huh, he wants you an' me strung up without any evidence or trial. That makes him bad enough by my reckoning.'

Clint nodded in agreement.

'When he turns up tomorrow he's gonna have the law on his side but there's only one thing that makes it so.'

The Mexican grinned at Clint's words. They had arrived at the temporary solution together and so deep was their understanding that no further words were necessary.

Dyer and Stacey were just finishing their chore when the pards made their way outside. There was a dust cloud rising to the north and the sound of a small herd on the run. Dyer nodded towards the dust.

'Here comes the rest of the outfit. Looks like they prised some steers outa the brush.'

The herd materialized out of the dust, about a hundred head of stringy bald-faced steers, all as wild as mountain cats and eager to put as many miles between them and the strange smell of man. They would have mingled with a big herd quickly enough but on their own they would take some handling for quite a time. The cowboys on the flanks rode hard to keep the beasts together and it was a skilful operation to guide the maddened animals to the fenced meadow where several sections of fencing had been removed to receive them. Even so, a dozen or so of the beasts raced the length of the entire meadow and skimmed over the fence, heading for the open range. It took another half an hour to catch up with them and get them safely coralled.

Tired and aching in every limb, the punchers slid out of their saddles, dusting themselves down before seeing to their horses. Dyer introduced them to the pards and they exchanged perfunctory nods. Only a couple of them displayed any real interest in the newcomers. They were both young, raw-boned men, who regarded the pards with steady appraisal from eyes that were calm and blue. Dyer introduced them as Rinty Denver and Con Levis.

'You sure hunted yourself a load of trouble, there Mister,' drawled Mex, nodding towards the corralled steers.

Dyer's face split into the first smile the pards had seen on it.

'Yeah, you're plumb right, Mex,' he agreed. 'But they sure make the credit side of my ledger look a bit healthier.' His smile disappeared. 'Not that they'll do me or Nugent much good come sun-up.'

'Don't worry too soon, Dyer,' Clint said. 'Maybe Dillon won't get to pressing things tomorrow. Anyway, my pard an' me are going to grab some shut-eye. Wake us an hour after sundown and have our cayuses saddled up ready. Get Johnny to pack us something and tell Nugent we'll be back before sun-up and we hope our ride'll be worth while.'

Dyer stared at the pards a long time wondering what to ask, then finally he just nodded towards the ranch house.

'Doss down in the first room on the left, upstairs,' he said.

The pards thanked him and went indoors. The bedroom contained two beds, and removing their boots and gunbelts Clint and Mex relaxed comfortably on top of the beds. Within minutes they were both fast asleep.

A couple of hours after sundown they

were crossing the line on to Bar Q range. The half moon slid into the sky at that precise moment shedding a thin light over the undulating grass. Mex glanced across to the east and pursed his lips.

'I reckon we could've done without that,' he remarked.

'Yeah, it's gonna make things a mite difficult,' his pard agreed. 'It'll be near as light as day when we get to the Bar Q.' Clint scanned the sky for clouds and sniffed the air in the hope of picking up the smell of rain, but he was a couple of months too early and gave it up.

Making use of every rise and fold in the ground they guided their mounts inexorably nearer and nearer the Bar Q headquarters. A few times they froze in the shadows while a puncher on night trick rode by hunched in the saddle, his slicker drawn tightly around him to withstand the night chill, and humming a tune to humour his edgy charges. Then at last they dismounted on the edge of a ring of red cedar and looked down upon Dillon's ranch house. Like most ranch houses it was an L-shaped, double-storied building with stables, smithy and washhouse strung out alongside, then on the opposite side the long bunkhouse and the corral forming a wide square or courtyard.

As they watched, a rider set out from the stables heading south, no doubt on his way to take over a section of range, then a silence settled down except for the incessant background chant of the cicadas. Now and then a hunting coyote howled a blood-chilling cry, but below men slept.

Leaving their mounts they made their way down the slope like wraiths. A couple of horses nickered and stamped in the stables and the pards lay full length on the ground until the fidgeting stopped, then on they went until at last they were alongside the house.

'Y' know Clint, it's my bet Dillon's got the note all nice an' ready for sun-up,' Mex whispered. 'I can picture him reading it over and gloating a dozen times before hitting the hay.'

'Been thinking the same thing,' replied Clint. 'Ain't much doubt about which room he uses either.'

'Nope, I never knew a boss who didn't use the big room overlooking the corral.'

They moved quietly up on to the veranda and tiptoed to the door. It was locked with the key inside the lock. Clint glanced at his pard in some dismay but the Mexican was busy removing his bandana. He placed it under the door and worked it evenly inside the house, then with his clasp knife he pushed the key out of the lock. It fell with a clatter and the nickering and stamping started up again. The pards pressed up against the sides of the house but no one stirred and after a few minutes Mex drew out the bandana with the key riding safely on it. Half a minute later they were inside the house.

They paused by the door until their eyes were accustomed to the dark, then took careful stock of the room helped by the thin shaft of light filtering through the windows. The air was filled with the stale smell of tobacco smoke and raw spirit, and from upstairs steady rhythmic snores told them men were sleeping off the effects of the drink. Neither Clint nor Mex were prepared to take any chances on that account. They knew only too well that most punchers could sink a couple of bottles of rye and still wake up clearheaded at the first strange noise.

Carefully they crossed the room, through an open doorway and up the stairs. At the top of the stairway they paused. The snores came from two rooms to their right, but to the left where they guessed Dillon slept, everything was silent. Mex grasped the door handle gingerly and the pards muttered their thanks to whoever had oiled the hinges, and turned it with utmost care. The door opened noiselessly. For a moment they were framed in the doorway taking stock of the room, then they were inside.

A long window ran almost its entire length and the moon spread its light evenly over everything. Dillon lay in the middle of the big bed breathing steadily. His clothes were draped over a chair standing on the far side of the bed; his gun hung over the headboard. The furniture was big and chunky, standing four square on a thick Navajo rug, and as Dillon stirred, the pards were thankful for the rug that smothered the sound of their approach. If they had been moving over bare boards, by the time they had circumnavigated the big dressing table Dillon would have been awake to raise the alarm. As it was, his eyes opened as the pards came alongside the bed but before he had focused his gaze, Mex brought his gun-barrel down on his head with just enough force to render him insensible for a few minutes. Then while Clint moved around the bed at speed to where Dillon's range clothes lay, Mex stayed, watching over the man intently.

Clint slung Dillon's shirt and denims on the bed and went to work on the black Prince Albert the man favoured. A delighted grin spread over the Texan's face as he withdrew a buff envelope from the deep inside pocket. He moved nearer the window and took a document from it. There was no need for him to strain his eyesight reading the contents. Nugent's signature was scrawled in a big bold hand at the bottom of the page. Placing the document inside his shirt, he replaced the envelope in Dillon's pocket and returned the shirt and denims to the chair.

Mex watched Clint's actions with satisfaction. It was gratifying to find their hunch to be correct. With a last glance at the unconscious Dillon, he crossed with Clint to the doorway. They eased themselves through, then as Mex pulled the door quietly closed, another opened on the other side of the passage.

Clint had a brief glimpse of a man framed in the doorway and with lightning speed he leapt in and cut short the man's shout with a vicious punch to the adam's apple. He caught the man as he fell and lowered him gently to the ground.

'Nice work,' whispered Mex as Clint led the way downstairs. 'Hope the luck stays with us.'

They made their way quickly through the two rooms and back out into the night. Luck stayed with them. No sooner had they regained the ring of big cedars than riders came in off the southern range and clattered to a halt outside the bunkhouse. The pards swung into their saddles and headed through the trees on to the open range. With their mission accomplished and time on their side, they were able to utilise their exceptional skill in moving through enemy country unseen, and they crossed on to Nugent's territory without incident.

There was a light showing in the Triple Bar ranch house when they rode in. The door opened and Nugent and Dyer came through. With the moon strong they recognized the pards immediately and Nugent hurried down to them.

'Hiya, Nugent,' Clint said as he slid to the ground. 'Get any luck in Rawlins?'

Nugent shook his head. 'Nope I guess not. Can't say I had much hope anyway. It's a fair-sized chunk of dinero I'm wanting and I could hardly expect my friends to have that much lying around. I had a try though.'

Dyer came forward and took the horses over whilst Clint and Mex followed Nugent into the ranch house. Once inside their host nodded them to chairs and poured out drinks. It was apparent he was curious as to the nature of the business that had taken them riding, but felt unable to pry. Mex lit up a cheroot and cast a quizzical eye at him.

'How many hands are you left with now the chips are down?' he asked.

'Three and Dyer,' the Triple Bar chief answered with a rueful look. 'I told 'em how things stood when I got back an' most of 'em asked for their time. I just about had enough to square 'em.' He took a drink and gave the pards a candid look. 'If you fellers want to back out of your sayso to lend a hand, I guess you're entitled.'

Neither Clint nor Mex took offence. They

61

respected the man's offer to let them off their promise now that the heat was on. Clint rolled himself a smoke whilst considering just how much to say.

'I guess you're left with enough hands to nurse the herd you're running at the moment,' he said at length, and Nugent agreed tersely. Clint stood up and sent a quick glance towards Mex. 'Well, we're not aiming on backing out but we'd like to be working on our own when Dillon shows up.'

Mex tossed his drink down and got to his feet. Nugent eyed the pards with some misgiving showing on his face. They made for the door but at the opening they paused and turned to face Nugent.

'When Dillon shows up for the dinero, ask him "What dinero"?' Clint said slowly. 'And when he calls you all sorts of a maverick an' says the money owing on the note he holds, ask him "What note?" I've gotta notion he's gonna bluster a lot but still not produce the note.' The Texan paused to admire Nugent's puzzled expression. 'Just tell him you'll pay when the note's handed over.'

Nugent mouthed questions but no sound came. He looked at the pards and took heart from the broad smiles that split their faces. When they slipped back out into the night, he stood a long time in the same place and a wide smile spread over his own face.

'Can't be more than an hour to sun-up

Mex,' said Clint when they stood outside. 'That windbreak to the north seems the best spot for us.'

'Yeah, I reckon we'll be able to see an' hear anything that goes on from there.'

They went to the stables, almost bumping into Dyer who was just emerging. He stared at them as they started re-saddling the horses he had just stripped.

'Thought you were backing Nugent!' he said, his face hard.

'Yeah, but from a discreet distance,' Mex answered lightly. 'That Dillon's sure some humdinger.'

Dyer stood watching them as they prepared their mounts for the trail. Clint caught a glimpse of his face in the light of the lamp that hung from a nail in a crossbeam. He was surprised to see a smile of what seemed satisfaction on the man's face. Dyer stood aside and made no comment when at length the pards led their mounts outside. He still said nothing when they mounted and rode away to the north.

When half a mile away they swung off the trail and headed across the rough graze back to the windbreak, a thick cluster of cottonwoods and red cedar. They ground-hitched their horses and took up position on the fringe of the trees behind a fallen trunk. They had a clear view down on to the paddock and settled down to wait for sun-up.

Dillon was a man of his word and sure enough, when the first light of day strengthened the moon's pale light, the tattoo of hoofbeats sounded from the south.

'Sure are enough of 'em by the sound of things,' Mex remarked as he shifted his position and sighted his Sharps down on to the big compound.

Clint made no reply. He was staring through the thin light for first sight of the Bar Q men. He saw them amidst the dust just before they burst in upon the Triple Bar. The dust cleared and about twenty riders fanned out. Dillon sat a big bay gelding in the middle of the group; next to him was a tall, tow-headed man with his Stetson set well back on his head. Clint took him to be Don Lear, Dillon's segundo. A few riders moved around the compound checking up on possible hidden gunmen. They returned and gave the all right signal to Dillon who turned his attention on the ranch house.

'You there, Nugent?' he roared. 'Let's get this business done.'

The laughter rippled amongst his men, the wave of sound reaching the pards. There was a pause and the ranch house door crashed open. Nugent stepped out on to the edge of the veranda in full view of the pards. He stared at Dillon then looked around at the milling riders.

'What's this, a war party?' he asked.

'Could be.' Dillon's answer was curt. 'You got the money?'

'What money?' Nugent was bland.

'You know darned well what money, Nugent,' Dillon hooted. 'The money you had from me on the strength of this spread. An' now's the time to settle the note or get off my territory.'

There was a long pause with the only noise the fidgety stamping of the horses. Clint and Mex, with their rifles trained on the men below, felt the tension rise.

'You hand over that note, Dillon, an' I'll pay.' Nugent spoke quite calmly.

'You ain't got the money to pay?' There was a tinge of doubt in Dillon's voice.

'That means you didn't bring the note. Howcome you're so sure that I couldn't raise the ante?'

'Aw, quit gabbing,' bawled Dillon. 'You're just playing for time. You know darned well I'm not carrying the note. You or a couple of your men stole that note out of my pocket a few hours ago.' He removed his sombrero and pointed to the place on his head where congealed blood still showed. 'That's what the hombres did when they stole the note. When I find out who did it they're gonna pay mighty heavy.'

'I know nothing of that, Dillon,' Nugent replied. 'But I'm not paying anything without the note.'

Dillon looked around his men, then back to Nugent. 'The talking's done Nugent. Your gamble stealing that note don't amount to anything. The lawman Jarman knows darned well that today is settling day and these men are witnesses that you haven't settled. You just get your things together and get to hell off my range.'

'Your men an' mine can be witnesses to my telling you I'll pay when you produce the note.' Nugent's voice was hard and steady.

Dillon shook his head.

'Nope, I'm taking over. You pack your freight, Nugent, unless you want to make a fight of it.'

Hands strayed towards guns and the riders milling below the pards showed eagerness in every line as they fanned out in fighting order. Then the whole group froze. Seconds drained away without men or beasts moving so much as a muscle, and the morning air became filled with menace.

The pards sensed the impending action with accurate timing, and the sharp rifle shots that split the silence were a fraction of a second ahead of the build up Dillon needed. Dillon's sombrero went flying through the air with two neat holes in it; the man himself jerked bolt upright in the saddle in surprise. When the riders turned to stare towards the windbreak, Clint and

Mex were standing in full view, their smoking rifles trained upon them.

'Any of you fellers move and Dillon dies,' Clint called, then when they gave no indication of moving, 'Dillon stays until you hombres are off Nugent range. Anybody aiming to horn in will die along with Dillon. Now get moving!'

The riders looked at Dillon for guidance but he made no sign and one by one they moved out, straight backed and hands clear of their guns. The sound of hoofbeats faded while Dillon sat his horse, frozen faced and unyielding.

CHAPTER FOUR

'Mebbe you have got the money after all, Nugent,' Dillon said when Clint and Mex had come down the slope and taken up positions alongside the Triple Bar man. 'It looks to me like you're in tow with these hombres, an' it's plumb sure they robbed the bank an' murdered Rushland an' Cressy.'

Nugent shrugged the remark away and looked to the pardners for guidance.

'It's my guess they broke into the Bar Q an' stole the note too,' Dillon added.

'That's pure guesswork, Dillon, and we've only got your word that any note was stolen,' Clint said evenly. 'Anyway the main thing is you can't prove that Nugent owes you anything and if you move in against the Triple Bar you're gonna be outside the law.'

Dillon snorted his derision. 'The law's in my pocket here, fella,' he growled. 'Not that I'd worry anyway. You enjoy having the drop on me now. It's the last time. I've told you to get moving outa the territory Nugent. If you stay I guess it's your funeral and your next stop'll be Boot Hill.'

'What makes you think you'll keep outa Boot Hill if you start the lead flying?' Mex asked. 'Mebbe you'd do better to keep your lip buttoned and stay on your own side of the fence?'

Dillon's grey eyes stared back to Mex. There was a chilling light in them that would have caused a lesser man to shudder, but Mex stared back, a sardonic smile on his face.

'You all done talking?' Dillon asked at length.

Clint and Mex nodded and Nugent just stared back at him, tight lipped. Behind Nugent, Dyer and Stacey watched with interest. Dillon's eyes rested briefly on Dyer then, ignoring the rifles held steadily by the pards, hauled his big bay gelding around and rode slowly out of the compound the way he had come.

'As soon as that hombre gets over the skyline where his men are waiting he's gonna order them in here with guns blazing,' Clint said turning to Nugent. 'We'd better get ready for 'em.'

'Looks like your idea didn't pan out after all,' Nugent replied but Clint shook his head.

'I don't agree. Without that note Dillon won't press things too hard. It'll be no more than a warning of what's to come.' Clint rolled a smoke and eyed the buildings carefully, 'Me an' Mex'll take it from the bunkhouse. I reckon you fellers had better take both sides of the house.'

He looked to Nugent for his opinion; he in turn glanced at his men. Denver and Levis were well in the background behind Dyer and Stacey. They didn't look too eager and there was an odd expression on Dyer's face, but they all nodded their agreement.

Dillon passed out of sight and Mex motioned to Clint for haste. They hurried to the bunkhouse and took up positions at the windows at either side.

'Think they'll come, Clint?' asked Mex as he checked his weapon.

'Yeah, they'll come but I'll be surprised if they make a real fight of it this time. I reckon Dillon will take time out to think things over a bit. It's more likely he'll make his mind up we've got the note and make a dead set at us. He can turn the heat on Nugent any time he likes.'

Clint had no sooner finished speaking than the sound of rapid hoofbeats told them the attack was on its way. Mex came to where Clint watched the riders burst over the skyline and split in two parties.

'Gonna take us from both sides,' observed Mex. His face was grim. 'If they get close enough I'll be shooting to hurt.' He moved back to his place on the other side of the bunkhouse.

Even though they were well out of range the riders were firing their revolvers in the general direction of the ranch house. Clint sighted along his Remington and took the first pressure, then relaxed. The man in his sights was firing his revolver into the air.

Down the grade the riders came and through the compound, firing at random. A return fire was coming from the ranch house and the pards heard cries of pain. The two parties rejoined just below the windbreak and this time the tall, tow-headed man who must have been Lear, Dillon's segundo, harangued his men. The pards could see that whatever orders Dillon had issued, they were now about to be countermanded. This time when the Bar Q spurred their horses there was a purposeful air about them and they were holding their fire.

Mex thrust his rifle aside and spun a Colt into his hand. He went to the door and pushed it open. Clint had the same thoughts. There was something inhuman about using the rifle against men armed only with side-arms. He joined Mex at the door.

The cavalcade of horsemen swept through, sending volley after volley thudding into the ranch buildings. Pressed tightly against the door frame, the pardners picked off a couple of men apiece who thudded to the ground. At the bottom of the grade the riders turned again in a cloud of dust but the pards had now run clean out of scruples, and slamming the door shut they took up their rifles, pushed the glass out of a couple of frames, and sent bullets flying into the huddle of men. Two more men fell and another shrieked in pain. Then the Bar Q men turned tail and spurred their horses up the grade.

The acrid smell of cordite hung in the early morning atmosphere as Clint and Mex left the bunkhouse and crossed the compound. Mere glances at the men lying in the dust confirmed they were dead and the pards wasted no time on them. Nugent came to the doorway with blood trickling down his face from a slight head wound. He had a shaken look on his face.

'They've gone,' he said woodenly. 'But young Stacey's dead.'

Clint and Mex followed him back inside. The other three men were gathered around Stacey's body and stepped aside to allow the pards to see the Bar Q men's handiwork. The blood still seeped out of a bullet hole in the dead youngster's forehead.

'That's mighty tough,' Clint growled. 'He was a mite young to die. Dillon's sure got something to answer for now.'

Nugent nodded. 'The law's gonna back Dillon,' he said ruefully. 'As far as I know Jarman is a straight shooter but he's mighty thin on reasoning, and having you already listed as bank robbers and killers, he'll take the fact you're siding me as a sure sign Dillon's in the right.'

'I think it's high time Jarman got his facts

right about us,' Mex put in. 'Is there a tele-graph office at Rawlins?'

Nugent shot him a surprised look. 'Yeah, at the Fargo office,' he replied.

'Then I'll tote Jarman in and get a mess-age to Jed Delahay.'

The Triple Bar men looked at Mex in amazement but Clint grinned and agreed.

'Give me a hand to get these cadavers outside on their cayuses and I'll tote 'em into Twin Springs.'

They went outside and manhandled the dead men on to three Bar Q horses that stood with lead reins dragging, then Mex climbed to the windbreak to collect his pinto and Clint's dun gelding. Down in the compound he picked up the lead rein of the first horse. The other two horses were tethered to the saddle cantle.

'I reckon you'd be smart to get some shut-eye Clint,' he suggested. 'Dillon'll be back but the next time he moves in it'll be at night. With luck I'll be back by then.'

Mex shook the reins and the pinto moved off, the three horses bearing their grisly burdens following in a string.

'Waal, for pure gall, he sure takes the prize,' Dyer said in wide-eyed astonishment.

'Yeah, that's for sure,' the raw-boned Rinty Denver put in. 'But he might find Jarman'll be a hard man to push around.'

Clint shrugged his shoulders and led his

74

gelding away to the stables. When he got back the other men were carrying Stacey's body outside. He joined the little cortege and took a hand in the burial on a knoll overlooking the ranch house.

'I guess I'll have to leave you an' your men to the chores, Nugent,' Clint said as they were nearing the ranch house on the return journey. 'I'll get that shut-eye my pard mentioned.'

'I'll get Jonny Sing to rustle up some breakfast,' Nugent replied. 'You'll need to eat before hitting the hay.'

The Triple Bar man wondered when he might get some shut-eye again himself but he was quick to realize that the Texan would serve him best by being in peak condition, and in any case Bellamy was not on the payroll as a working hand.

Clint did not waste too much time on eating, just taking enough to placate the eager Chinese cook who hovered around appraising his every expression. He went up to the bedroom and throwing his clothes on a chair climbed into bed.

Mex Juarez hauled his pinto to a halt and gazed through the shimmering heat haze down on Twin Springs. It was no longer a ghost town. Puffs of dust spurted up as riders moved in and out of town and there was a general air of life about it.

75

He fished for a cheroot and bit the end off thoughtfully. Entering a town empty save for the marshal and Rushland's daughter was one thing, but moving in toting six dead men with the town bustling with humanity was another, and one that needed thought. Mex smoked his way through the cheroot then turned his horse off the trail, taking to the rough ground that skirted the hills bordering Twin Springs.

By careful use of the terrain he got to within a quarter of a mile of the town. He slipped out of the saddle and untied the lead rein of the first horse from his saddle cantle. He slipped the lead rein off then slapped the animal hard on the rump. With a start the horse moved off trailing the other two along. They had the scent of town and stabling, and nothing would stop them now from making their entry.

The Mexican watched them until he was sure they would enter town from the north, then he remounted and worked his way around to the south trail. He waited his time before entering town, choosing just the moment the excitement broke and men started running to see what all the noise was about. No one noticed him ride in. He dismounted alongside the gaolhouse and tethered his pinto to the hitch-rail on the opposite side of the street. Marshal Jarman was just pushing through the fringe of the crowd surrounding the three Bar Q Horses and Mex smiled his satisfaction.

Crossing the street he climbed to the sidewalk and pushed the gaolhouse door open. His eyes opened in surprise, then he swept his sombrero off his head and bowed to the lovely girl who stared back at him in alarm. Mex shut the door behind him and moved into the centre of the office. He eyed the girl with undisguised approval. She was worthy of his or any other man's attention. The black habit she wore contrasted delightfully with her ash blonde hair and peach pink skin, and her finely-moulded features were dominated by big deep-blue eyes fringed with jet-black eyelashes.

'Don't be alarmed, Ma'am,' Mex said. 'Just take a seat. You can keep me company until Jarman comes back.'

The girl backed against the table and pointed an accusing finger at him.

'You're one of the two men who killed my father,' she cried and rushed towards the door. Mex caught her and stifling her struggles, led her back to the chair.

'Miss Rushland,' he said, an unwonted air of seriousness on his handsome face. 'Believe me, my pardner and I had no part in the murder of your father. My whole reason for being here now is to convince Jarman of that fact, but I'd like to express my sorrow in your bereavement.'

The girl calmed and stared searchingly at the debonair Mexican. She nodded slowly and the colour came back into her face.

'I believe you. You don't look as though you'd kill in cold blood.'

'Thank you, Ma'am.' Mex bowed again. 'Matt Nugent thought the same way. He was quite happy to offer us the refuge of his spread.' He watched her carefully for reaction, and the way her hand went to her throat at mention of Nugent's name told him plenty. 'It's too bad that Nugent will be looking for refuge himself mighty soon.'

The girl was wide-eyed at once. 'Nugent will?' she asked.

Mex nodded. 'Yeah, your father was holding Nugent's money to pay off the note Dillon held on the Triple Bar. The money's gone and Dillon's aiming on taking over Nugent's spread.'

He paused, measuring the effect of his words, but the girl's thoughtful face gave no sign. Things had gone quiet up the street and Mex crossed to the door, listening intently.

'I guess Jarman'll be back pretty soon,' he said. 'I might have to rush him a bit because he figures I'm a killer. Just don't get alarmed.'

'What was all the excitement about anyway?' the girl asked.

Mex gave her a straight look. 'Dillon's men tried rushing Nugent off his spread this morning,' he announced. 'Some men got killed and I toted 'em in for burial.'

She turned her face aside but Mex could still see her shocked expression. Heavy footfalls sounded along the sidewalk and Mex raised his fingers to his lips, warning the girl to remain silent. He backed alongside the door, his gun held nonchalantly. The door banged open and Jarman stomped inside.

'Sorry I had to leave you, Miss Kathy,' he said, then stopped as he interpreted the implication of her look. He swung around to look down the muzzle of the Mexican's gun. He made a half-hearted attempt to go for his own gun then allowed his hands to drop to his side.

'You've sure got gall feller,' he said. 'What in heck are you after?'

'You, Jarman!' Mex eased himself from the wall and pushed the door shut with his foot. 'You're too allfired stiff-necked to listen to anything my pard and I might say to clear us of the murder of Miss Rushland's father so I'm totin' you into Rawlins and you can send a telegraph to Sheriff Delahay of Butte, Montana. I reckon he'll put you straight were we stand.'

Jarman's burly frame stiffened and he stared in disbelief at Mex, but the cold light that had taken the place of the gentle mockery in the Mexican's eyes chased his disbelief away. He swallowed hard.

'You've sure set yourself some chore,' he

79

growled. 'What makes you think you'll get me to Rawlins?'

Mex moved up close.

'That's no problem,' he said calmly. 'It's up to you whether you want a comfortable ride or make it draped over a saddle.'

He took out his other gun and spun it so that he held the barrel. There was no mistaking his intention and Jarman blanched.

'I'll get saddled up,' he snarled.

The Mexican's eyes bored into him. 'Now that's good sense Jarman. Just unbuckle that gunbelt and stand over there against the wall.'

The marshal did as he was told and Mex flashed a look at Kathleen Rushland, who was watching with bated breath. His quick smile reassured her. Taking up the gunbelt, he unloaded the guns and replaced the long-handled Colts back in their holsters. He tossed the gunbelt back to the red faced marshal.

'Just get this straight, Jarman. You'll ride outa town like you want to. Any false move and I'll drill you so that you'll do no more riding. Now get moving and saddle up your cayuse.'

Jarman did not argue. He rebuckled his gunbelt and led the way through the cell block to the stable at the back. Mex bowed to the girl as he passed her and gave her a smile of compassion. The grief she suffered through the death of her father showed only too clearly in her lovely eyes.

Mex watched carefully while the marshal saddled up a big white-faced paint mare, then instructed the man to lead the animal around the side of the gaol where his own pinto waited. They mounted and left the town side by side as though they were pards of long standing. Jarman was convinced the Mexican would shoot without hesitation and in consequence took no chances.

They rode in silence for a long time, just the creaking of saddle leather and the jingle of Jarman's spurs, and all the time Jarman's curiosity was mounting.

'Howcome you reckon this Delahay will speak up for you an' that Bellamy hombre?' he asked at length.

'We've been pards a long time,' replied Mex simply. 'We've burned a lot of trails together an' cleaned up a lot of territory on the way. I guess he can also tell you we've no call to rob banks since we've gotta stake in the Randall-Houston combine in Montana that pays us plenty.'

Jarman eased his mount to a stop and Mex reined in.

'I've heard plenty 'bout Delahay,' Jarman said. 'An' I scouted alongside Rod Houston with a wagon train on the Oregon trail before he took to punchin' cows. You say you worked for his outfit?'

81

'Yeah, still on the payroll,' Mex agreed. 'Just heading south to visit my folk, then back to Montana.'

The marshal rubbed his face with a horny hand. 'If Delahay gives you a clean bill, are you aiming to head straight on south?'

Mex shook his head. 'Nope. Bellamy and me are plumb curious to know who did murder the banker and his pard, and why the town was empty when we rode in. I guess we'll stay around until we know the answers.'

He lit a cheroot and studied the lawman's face through the smoke. Jarman's brow was creased with the effort of thought, then the suspicion flooded back.

'You showed up in town just when those broncs toted in six dead men. Bar Q men. You have any hand in that?'

Mex shrugged. 'Don't think I killed more'n two of 'em,' he answered quietly and grinned when Jarman stared. 'Dillon started throwing lead at the Triple Bar this morning. Me an' my pard chipped in with Nugent. Considering the odds were about six to one, the score was even. Young Stacey got salivated.'

'Dillon's within his rights taking over the Triple Bar if Nugent hasn't paid up on that note,' Jarman growled. 'But I reckon he could lay off until we get a lead on who robbed the bank.' He looked long and hard at Mex. 'You aiming to keep siding Nugent?'

Mex drew hard on his cheroot before answering. 'It could be,' he said. 'Mebbe we'll get to helping you find the killers but by my reckoning that'll still leave us siding Nugent.'

'Waal, I guess I can take your sayso Juarez,' Jarman said. 'There's no call for us to ride into Rawlins.'

'Nope. My sayso's not good enough now Jarman. You might be convinced now but if anything else pops up on this range, you might get to doubting and try clapping us in the hoosegow just when we can't afford to be tied down.'

The marshal gave way with bad grace. 'Have it your way,' he growled and spurred his horse into action. Mex grinned at the lawman's display of bad temper and urged his pinto into a run after him.

'How come Twin Springs was empty when we rode in?' he asked when he caught up.

The marshal looked across at him as though somehow he held Mex and Clint responsible in some measure for the exodus from Twin Springs. Grudgingly he told Mex the story of the sourdough and how the townsfolk had moved out en masse to stake a claim in a fortune. Some men were still prospecting the area but most were back in Twin Springs, angry and thirsting to get their hands on the man who had fooled them.

'Mighty good way of clearing a town ready

83

for a bank robbery,' Mex commented. 'But it strikes me someone was behind that move who knew exactly what the bank was holding. Any passing gang would have just rode in an' made a snatch, mebbe by night. You tried trailing that sourdough?'

'That's what I'd be doing right now,' Jarman stated pointedly.

Mex let the remark pass and for the rest of the journey the two men rode in silence. At the Wells Fargo office they dispatched a telegraph dictated by Mex to Sheriff Delahay of Butte County, Montana. It took a couple of hours for the message to be relayed via four other staging depots and for the reply to go through the same channels. They were lucky that Delahay was on hand to reply at once. The telegraphist made to hand the reply to Mex who refused it and indicated Jarman. The marshal took the message and read it slowly. There was a new light of respect in his eyes when he looked up at Mex.

'You want to read it?' he asked but Mex declined.

'Delahay sure rates you high, Juarez,' Jarman continued. 'An' that goes for Bellamy too. I guess you're a coupla straight shooters.'

'Sure glad that's settled,' Mex replied. 'An' now I'll get back to the Triple Bar.'

He left the office rapidly. Now that Jarman was satisfied he wasn't particularly keen on the man's company. He was astride his pinto and heading out of town before the marshal reached the sidewalk.

When Mex and the Marshal left the gaol-house Kathleen Rushland stayed on for quite a time, undecided as to her course of action. The thought of Lew Dillon and Matt Nugent fighting appalled her. Both men interested her tremendously and each in turn had made it abundantly clear that they wanted her interest to become exclusive. Kathleen was in no hurry to make up her mind. She valued the friendship and company of both men and shelved the thought that one day she would have to let her feelings for one of them deepen.

It was with surprise that she now found her concern was for Matt Nugent only. She did not try to reason things out. It became imperative all at once that Nugent should come to no harm. Thrusting aside thoughts of her personal distress she hurried outside into the searing sunshine and on to the stable at the rear of her house. Saddling up her mild-mannered white mare she headed out of town in the direction of the Bar Q.

She started her ride at an easy pace but a sense of urgency stole over her and she pushed the mare harder and harder so that when she finally hauled the animal to a stop outside the Bar Q headquarters, it was running with sweat and blowing hard. Lew

Dillon came to the door as she climbed out of the saddle. He looked at her in some surprise and took in the condition of her mount. He came down the three steps to greet her.

'You've sure pressed that cayuse, Kathy,' he said. 'What in heck made you travel so fast?' He nodded to a man who had come forward from a knot of punchers. 'See to the horse, Slim,' he barked, then placing one arm around the girl's shoulder he led her up to the house.

Settling the girl down in a leather armchair Dillon went into the kitchen and brought back a jug of applejack. He poured out a glass and handed it to the girl, then stood with his back to the wide fireplace looking at her.

'I – I heard about the gunplay this morning at the Triple Bar, Lew,' she said after taking a long drink. 'What's the reason for it?'

Dillon's handsome face darkened and he weighed his words.

'Matt Nugent's been running his spread on my money for a long time,' he said. 'Today was settling day. He didn't settle an' he wasn't ready to move out. I guess my men decided they'd encourage him to move. Anyway there was some gunplay as you said.'

'He was going to pay, Lew. My father was

looking after the money for him. Matt can't be blamed for what happened at the bank. Surely you can give him a chance to raise the money again?'

Dillon shook his head. 'He's had time enough Kathy. I can't afford to give him any more time. He'd never get on his feet enough to pay me back and I can't carry a weak neighbour. Sooner or later someone will push him outa business and mighty soon they'd be pushing me.'

Kathy's eyes opened wide and she gazed up at the man in surprise.

'There's nothing weak about Matt,' she said firmly. 'And well you know it. Anyhow as soon as things get sorted out at the bank he might get back what was lost.'

It was Dillon's turn to be surprised.

'What do you mean?' There was a harsh note to his voice that did not escape the girl.

'Just that Rushland's like to honour their obligations and if I'm left with enough, I shall do so.'

'But Nugent wasn't a depositor,' Dillon expostulated. 'Your father was just keeping it for him with no business strings. I reckon you'll find it tough enough making good the money lost by depositors.'

Kathy didn't answer for a long time. There was truth enough in what Dillon had said.

'I'm not forgetting we were holding money of yours, Lew,' she said at length and spots of colour flamed high on his cheeks.

'I wouldn't hold you to be repaying that,' he growled. 'But I'd sure want it before it could be used to help Nugent.' He noticed her glass was empty and refilled it, then sat down in the chair opposite her. For some moments he looked at her, the girl's lovely features and flawless figure making his blood run hotter.

'How come you're carrying a banner for Nugent?' he asked. 'You know the way of the west, Kathy. If a man fails he goes under.'

The girl nodded. 'Sure, I know the way of things but you can't say Matt Nugent failed. I'd say he's had mighty bad luck.'

'Yeah, he's had bad luck. I reckon I had bad luck too, lending him the dinero in the first place.' He shrugged his shoulders. 'And what do I get instead? A rundown spread that'll cost me plenty before I start to see a return.'

The girl stood up and stared at Dillon. Her blouse strained under the stress of her emotion and the man had difficulty in dragging his eyes up to her face.

'Lew!' she cried. 'Now that my father's dead you and Matt are my only real friends. I don't want either of you to be hurt.'

Dillon stood up and came close to her. She could see his thoughts reflected in his eyes and more than ever she realized she could never go with him voluntarily along the paths his mind had already plumbed. The man's next words took away the element of choice if she wanted to save Nugent from losing his spread and to keep him alive.

'I know the way you feel Kathy an' I'd sure like to oblige but you can't expect me to go along with your wishes because you count Nugent as your friend. Now if you were my wife things would be different and I'd be more likely to take a tolerant view of things.'

He drew her close and despite herself she could not help but thrill to the strength and eagerness of the man. She steeled herself and shook her head when he made to kiss her.

'No – not now, Lew,' she panted. 'This is no time for me to think of happiness. I must get back to town. I have my father's funeral to arrange.'

Dillon's breath hissed as he allowed his pent-up feelings to ease off and he held her away from him.

'Yeah, I guess you're right,' he said. 'I reckon you'll have to forgive me for forgetting. You're that durned pretty you chase all other thoughts away.'

'You'll come in tomorrow, Lew?' she asked struggling to regain her composure.

The man nodded but his eyes were fastened on the swift rise and fall of her breasts.

'And you won't carry on the fighting

against the Triple Bar before I see you?'

Dillon checked the answer that came first to his mind. He could promise anything. He could take care of Nugent without implicating himself. No point in antagonizing her when he wanted her so badly.

'If that's how you want it, Kathy,' he agreed. 'But you'll sure have to marry me mighty soon if you want to keep influencing my judgment.'

'Don't rush me, Lew,' she breathed. 'I must have time to think things out.'

She gathered up her gloves and hat and started for the door. Dillon came up behind her and they went on to the veranda together. He yelled to a man to bring her horse. Lear was watching a puncher break-in a strawberry mustang and Dillon called him over.

'See Miss Kathy gets back to town all right Don,' he said.

Lear let his eyes rest briefly on the girl as he nodded, but in that split second she felt a shudder of revulsion run through her and despite the boiling heat of the sun she felt cold.

CHAPTER FIVE

Clint woke up with the vague feeling that someone had been in the room. The sunlight was still streaming through the window and by the angle of the rays he decided he had not slept for more than two hours. He was about to dismiss the matter when he remembered the document in the inside pocket of his slicker lying across the back of a chair.

Jumping out of bed he felt inside the pocket. The note was gone. His first impulse was to dress and rush downstairs in the hope of catching the culprit but he let the moment pass. Instead he sat on the edge of the bed and rolled himself a smoke. He was halfway through his second cigarette when he heard the shod horse canter out of the compound. Crossing swiftly to the window he saw the unmistakable square figure of Dyer astride a light grey mare.

Stabbing out the cigarette the Texan lay back on the bed and relaxed. Characteristically he shelved all thoughts of Dyer's defection. He had learned the only way to recharge his agile mind and body was to rest completely whenever he could. He allowed two hours to slip away, then feeling refreshed he dressed and went downstairs. Johnny Sing had a pot of coffee brewing in the kitchen and when the Texan looked in he filled a mug and handed it over.

'Mighty good brew, Johnny,' Clint said. 'I'd sure be obliged if you'd rustle up a pack for me. I'm hitting the trail an' it'll mebbe gone nightfall before I get back.'

The Chinaman pointed with a cleaver to the big sideboard where some packs were already made up.

'Help yourself,' he invited then turned his attention to the meal he was preparing.

Clint finished his coffee and taking a pack, went on outside. Nugent, Denver and Levis were at the far end of the big meadow repairing a section of fence that one of the wild brush steers had broken. He did not attempt to attract their attention but went on into the stables. Saddling up his big dun gelding he led it outside and climbing into the saddle, headed his mount in the direction Dyer had taken.

The Texan encountered no trouble in picking up the segundo's trail. It led first to the north then veered around out of sight of the ranch headquarters to the south. Straight as a die it went then for the Bar Q.

Clint allowed his mount to pick its own speed. He was in no hurry. When Dyer's trail passed over into Bar Q territory he turned off and headed for the hills. Setting his mount to the grade, he worked his way deep into Dillon's range. Every now and again he paused and scoured the undulating grassland. Dillon's range was certainly well stocked. Large herds were dotted around line camps and Clint could just pick out the punchers riding through the shimmering haze.

Once when the haze lifted completely he had a clear view of the river that came out of the hills and ran through Bar Q and Triple Bar country. The sun glinted along its length, showing it running deep into the Bar Q then when well into Triple Bar territory, meandering back almost to the foot of the hills then veering diagonally towards the north-east and the hills that ranged over Twin Springs.

'Mighty good range,' Clint muttered aloud. 'No chance of running short of water. So that rules out one reason why Dillon wants the Triple Bar.'

He rode on until at last the Bar Q headquarters came into view, just a huddle of what seemed tiny boxes in the distance. He dismounted and squatting on his heels, rolled himself a smoke, keeping the ranch buildings under close observation. He waited about half an hour then a dot moved out from the buildings, dust rose up in the wake of the moving dot, and Clint decided the dot was a horse and rider. He reckoned he knew who the rider was. Climbing back into the saddle the Texan headed back the way he had come but always he kept the distant rider in view.

They were still on Bar Q territory when the rider made a wide detour to avoid a herd that was moving slowly south. He came quite close to the base of the hills. As Clint expected it was Dyer, squat and solid looking and one would have thought, utterly dependable. Clint's lips curled in distaste as he watched the man ride on back towards the Triple Bar.

He was about to follow when away to the east he saw a knot of men driving about fifty head of cattle into a coulee. Smoke rose out of the coulee from a newly made fire. With his interest aroused Clint studied the terrain closely with the hope of getting close enough to the scene of activity without being seen. It was possible to ride to within about four hundred yards from the coulee but from that point he would only be able to proceed by wriggling through the long grass.

Steering his horse down a long gully he reached the foot of the hills at a level lower than the lip of the coulee, then choosing his route with caution he made his way to the point he had selected to ride his animal.

Easing out of the saddle and leaving the lead rein trailing, Clint crawled forward inch by inch until eventually he lay peering down on the scene of sweating activity below.

Three men were busy roping steers; one kept the irons going in the fire and another, the running iron artist, was blocking out the Bar Q brand and adding Nugent's brand. The Triple Bar. As Clint watched the punchers released a newly branded steer. It struggled to its feet, bawling, and joined the rebranded group.

'Three more Cluny,' yelled the burly man with the running iron, 'an I reckon that'll do.'

Cluny waved his acknowledgement and edged his horse near enough to a white-faced steer to rope it unerringly with his lariat. The steer ran on guided by the other men until near the fire, then when the rope tightened, Cluny and the other two punchers held it down while the man with the branding irons got busy. The acrid smell of scorching hair and hide reached Clint. The steer gave voice and struggled up when the ropes were slipped.

Time was getting short and the Texan slid away from the edge of the coulee. There was enough noise coming from the coulee so that he reckoned he was safe to move freely, and he ran down to where his gelding waited. He was almost back up to the timber line when the steers and riders burst out of the coulee and made for the Triple Bar boundary.

Clint reined in at the top of the gully and watched the steers driven deep into Triple Bar territory. The riders eventually dismounted in a dry wash and the Texan set his horse moving again to keep tabs on their movements. Smoke curled up out of the dry wash then after a few moments it died away. The men remounted their horses and the dust spurted as they headed back for the Bar Q.

The Texan watched Dillon's men as they crossed back on to Bar Q territory and pushed on as though intent on returning to headquarters. He waited until there was no danger of being observed then he kneed his gelding into action. Down the grade the animal went as sure-footed as a mountain goat, then on towards the dry wash.

'Huh, so that's it,' Clint growled as he slid out of the saddle and gazed at the remains of the fire Dillon's men had made. The block and running iron lay beside the blackened embers. He lit a cigarette and smoked as he considered his next move, then stubbing out the end, he cleared away all trace of the fire, and stuck the branding irons in his saddle roll.

The Bar Q steers had strung out a bit and for the next hour Clint sweated, bunching them together and getting them moving in the desired direction. It took him another hour to get them back to the coulee where some of them had been rebranded, then with a grin of satisfaction he turned away from the steers and made for the Triple Bar.

With Rawlins well behind him, Mex settled his pinto down to a steady pace and allowed his mind to play around with Nugent's dilemma. He was convinced that in some way all that happened in Twin Springs, the sourdough with the story of a big gold strike, and the bank robbery, had connections with Dillon's desire to take over the Triple Bar. He could not believe that Kathleen Rushland was the reason behind Dillon's determination to edge Nugent out. Dillon was after bigger stakes.

There was no easy solution so Mex gave it up and contented himself with one of his evil-smelling cheroots. One thing gave him satisfaction: he and Clint could ride into Twin Springs any time now without looking over their shoulders.

He was just a few miles away from Twin Springs when his quick eyes picked up the unmistakable hoofmarks of a burro where a defile led off the trail. At one point the dust was completely undisturbed by the wind and the marks showed up as plainly as when first made. Mex eyed the defile with interest. It was Bar Q territory. Without hesitation he turned his pinto into the opening and set it to the grade. Here and there up the narrow twisting defile he picked up the burro's trail mingled with the hoofmarks of a shod horse, and at length he emerged at the top where it opened out into a shallow grass-covered valley.

Mex dismounted and left his pinto to graze while he scouted around. The signs were pretty clear to him. He saw where a fire had been made and where a number of horses had been picketed, then on one side of the valley, beside a big bald boulder, he looked down on what was left of the burro. Its white skeleton lay picked clean by the buzzards and other carrion.

At the far end of the valley another defile led down to the Bar Q side of the hill and here he found evidence enough that riders had entered from Dillon's spread and left the valley the same way. He returned to where he had left his pinto and after allowing it to graze for another quarter of an hour or so, climbed back into the saddle and left the valley by way of the second defile, deep into Bar Q country.

When he rounded the last bend and gained a clear view of the nearby grassland he saw a puncher who was heading south towards a group of cows. The puncher saw Mex at the same time and hauled his cowpony around to face the newcomer. Mex carried right on giving the impression he intended to ignore the existence of the Bar Q man.

'Just stay where you are hombre!' shouted the puncher when Mex was still about fifty yards away.

The Mexican reined in and eyed the puncher blandly.

'What's eating you?' he asked.

The man edged his horse in closer. He held a long barrelled Colt with the air of a man who would find pleasure in using it. There was the light of recognition in the man's eyes and Mex grinned back as he also recognized the man as having been one of the five who had pursued Clint and himself a couple of days ago.

'I kinda thought we'd meet again greaser,' the puncher sneered. 'Looks like you're gonna go back to town after all to swing for that bank steal.'

'You're a bit late feller,' Max replied easily. 'My pard an' I have been squared on that account. If it wasn't for the fact I ain't too keen on Jarman, we'd be buddies.'

The man's expression did not change and his gun pointed just as steadily at the Mexican's midriff.

'That's as maybe, but I don't go along with Jarman. He's a mite slow on the uptake. Mebbe when I tote you in draped over that cayuse o' your'n he'll change his mind again.'

'You're sure setting yourself up some chore.' The banter had dropped away from

Mex and his eyes glinted with a malevolent light. 'If you want to go on living hombre, you'd better slide that smokepole back into your holster.'

The puncher's eyes opened in astonishment. Either this Mexican had a lot of gall or else he was a gun artist of outstanding caliber. He watched Mex slide his feet out of the stirrups before he willed himself to test the Mexican's ability.

In the split second that the puncher's finger tightened on the trigger, Mex slid sideways out of the saddle. Before he hit the ground his gun was out. Three times the Bar Q man's gun roared, the bullets missing the moving target by yards, then Mex fired, just once, and eased himself to his knees to watch the long barrelled Colt fall out of the puncher's nerveless fingers to hit the ground just in front of the man who had staked his life on its use.

Mex got to his feet and crossed to the man's side. Gently he turned him over but the need for gentleness had gone. The bullet had passed clean through his heart. An expression of regret flitted across the Mexican's face. 'Why in heck did every hombre have to be so gun crazy,' he thought, as he slid his gun back into its holster.

Although the dead man was hefty, Mex hauled him up across the saddle with an ease that spoke volumes for his wiry strength.

Tethering the corpse safely he took hold of the lead rein, and calming the horse that shied from the smell of blood, remounted his pinto. Before moving off he lit one of his cheroots, drawing in the harsh smoke deeply, thankful that he was still around to enjoy it.

'Reckon I'll take you back to your boss,' he said at length and he gazed speculatively at the corpse as though expecting it to reply. Stubbing out his cheroot he set off for the Bar Q. It was his intention to get as close as possible to the ranch headquarters then send the laden horse in on its own.

Kathleen Rushland tried keeping her mare just ahead of Don Lear's mount as they rode past the corrals on to the Twin Springs trail. There was something about her companion that chilled her blood and gave her a kind of mental paralysis. His eyes had rested on her as she climbed into the saddle and she felt almost naked under his scrutiny. When she returned his glance with all the hostility she could muster, the smouldering depths seemed to engulf her and she felt unnerved and so weak that she trembled violently. The way his lip curled in derision and full knowledge of his power did nothing to help.

When the man turned his back on her and spurred his Texan paint horse into action, she came back to her senses and told herself she was merely being foolish, and after considering that Lear would do nothing to place himself in jeopardy with Dillon, she kneed her mount after him.

For a couple of miles they rode with Lear in the lead but Kathy found something so magnetic about the man that she could not take her eyes from him. This she concluded was an evil thing and determined to sever his power, she urged her mount out in front. Lear's cold eyes followed her and his mind slid away from his scheming to dwell on the girl's trim figure. He had never considered women worth the trouble they caused and in the ordinary course of events would not have looked twice at Kathleen Rushland, but her stiff necked manner irked him. The way she relegated him to underling status with a glance set his dislike smouldering into something deeper and he felt an irresistible urge to treat her roughly, to take the starch out of her, in fact to make her crawl.

He reckoned she felt safe, confident that he was in fear of Dillon as indeed most men on this range were. His mouth split in an evil grin as he thought just how wrong she was in her assumption. He had plans for Dillon in due course and time would tell who was king-pin. Lear touched his paint horse with the spurs and drew alongside the girl.

'You're in an all-fired hurry, Ma'am,' he

sneered. 'What in heck's eating you?'

Kathy just sneaked a glance at him, gauging his attitude.

'I've got things to do in town,' she replied. 'But there's no need for you to tag along. If you don't like the pace why don't you go back?'

Lear reached over and held on to her mount's head. He hauled the two animals to a stop. His eyes smouldered as he looked at her.

'You'll go at my speed,' he snapped. 'An' don't get sassy with me or I'll take it out of your stiff-necked hide.'

Kathy's eyes opened wide in a mixture of surprise and horror. She averted her face in order that she would not have to look into the man's hypnotic eyes.

'Let me go!' she shouted. 'Let me go or my God, I'll ride right back and tell Lew Dillon about your behaviour.'

Lear leaned over and struck her across the face with his open hand. He smiled sourly at her shocked expression.

'When I've finished with you, you're welcome to hightail it back to Dillon but it's my guess you'll think twice before telling anyone, least of all Dillon, if you're set on gettin' wedded to him.'

Kathy tried to hit the man's restraining hand away from the reins but he held on, then with a vicious backhanded blow he hit her out of the saddle. He slid to the ground and advanced towards her. She sat up with blood trickling from a split lip, stark fear on her face. Lear's expression held no mercy and there was an eagerness about him that set the girl's hopes at the lowest possible ebb.

When the gunshot cracked and Lear's sombrero smacked to the ground with the bullet hole in it, Kathy was too bemused with shock to realize she was saved. Spinning round Lear clawed for his gun but the next bullet thudded the weapon out of his hand even before it had cleared leather. He stood, staring back with hate laden eyes at the Mexican astride the pinto who held his smoking gun with such nonchalant menace.

'Oh, am I glad to see you,' Kathy cried, scrambling to her feet.

'Mighty glad to be on hand, Ma'am,' Mex replied without taking his eyes off Lear. 'Now just get around that jasper slowly and take his other gun, then get back into the saddle.'

Kathy did as she was told, coming up behind Lear to take the gun out of his holster.

'Wa'al, what now?' Lear drawled. 'Looks like you've got the drop again. One of these days we'll meet on even terms then I reckon you'll get to Boot Hill on a shutter.'

'When the time comes I'll take my chances Mister,' replied Mex quietly. 'And the only reason I'm not putting a slug into your mangy guts now is that I'm looking forward to settling with you from an even start.'

'What's wrong with now?' Lear's expression showed that he did not have much hope of being accommodated but he felt it was worth a try. The Mexican for his part would have been only too pleased to oblige but consideration for the girl weighed too heavily. If he had the bad luck to be out-gunned then Kathleen Rushland would be left in no better circumstances than he had found her.

'You any great shakes with a gun, Ma'am?' Mex posed the question as the desire to get to grips with the woman-beater surged through him.

'I wouldn't miss from this range,' she replied bringing Lear's own gun to bear on the Bar Q man.

Giving the girl a satisfied nod Mex slipped his gun back into its holster and unbuckled his belt.

'Just aim to kill if this hombre bothers you, that's if he gets the good luck to lick me.' As he spoke Mex let his gunbelt drop and slid to the ground. Lear eyed him in some surprise then jumped in immediately to the attack.

The first vicious swing missed Mex by no more than a whisker and he only half-parried the next half dozen blows the Bar Q man flung at him. One thing was certain, Lear was some considerable battler.

Giving ground Mex countered with a couple of straight lefts to Lear's face, but although blood spurted from the man's mouth and nose he bored in, using fists, elbows and head. Twice in rapid succession Lear handed heavy rights to the Mexican's chin, causing him to hang on until his head cleared, then when Lear's confidence mounted and he pushed Mex away to measure the pay-off punch, the Mexican came back fast, flashing a solid blow on his opponent's nose.

Lear staggered and his eyes glazed when Mex followed up with a combination of vicious punches to the head and stomach. He clawed forward, managing to grasp his adversary, and held on. Both men went down and for a few moments they rolled, first one on top, then the other, trading punch for punch. All the time Kathy Rushland watched with mounting interest. Her spirits rose and fell with the tide of the battle but she was resolved to use the gun if it became necessary.

Breaking the Mexican's hold, Lear scrambled to his feet and aimed a savage kick at Mex's head. Twisting like a snake Mex evaded the kick and grasped Lear's foot, hurling him to the ground. Lear's head struck the butt of the gun Mex had shot out of his hand previously and the fight went out of him. Mex hauled him to his feet and for good measure planted another pile-driving blow into the man's face. Lear went down like a log and Mex staggered back to his pinto where he held on to the pommel for a while as his strength surged back.

'Some fight, eh?' he muttered more to himself than to the girl, then with his strength restored, he wiped the dust and sweat away from his face and dug out a cheroot.

With the cheroot going nicely, he picked up his gunbelt and refastened it, then untied the lead rein of the horse bearing the corpse from his own saddle cantle and tied it up to Lear's paint before climbing astride his pinto.

'Where now, Ma'am?' he asked, turning to Kathy.

'I was going back to town,' she answered, 'but if you're heading for the Triple Bar, I'll come along. I'd like to talk to Matt Nugent.'

'Triple Bar it is then,' Mex replied with a smile. 'We'll leave that carrion to come around on his lonesome.'

The girl gave one backward glance as they rode away and shuddered as the reaction set in.

CHAPTER SIX

It was a grim-faced crowd that gathered to watch the interment of Daniel Rushland, Abe Cressy the man who had died with him, and the six Bar Q men toted in by Mex. A notable exception was the under-sized mortician Dave Brock. He had collected his fees just before the cortege had left for Boot Hill and it added up to the best couple of days' business in his memory.

Dillon's interest in the dead Bar Q men ended when he paid Dave Brock and now he stood beside Kathleen Rushland, exuding solicitude for her. Matt Nugent stood at her other side, his mind only half on the cere-mony. He was conscious of the ring of Dil-lon's men, all eyeing him with the menace of those who were intent upon revenging their comrades.

Matt realized that he should have stayed away. It had been against his better judg-ment that he had ridden into town last night with Kathy, but once committed Nugent just could not turn back so he had stayed on for the funeral. He was conscious of the girl beside him who had to struggle for com-posure as Eli Rudd, the blacksmith, intoned the brief service. Her presence moved him tremendously and he cursed inwardly at the bad luck that had sent bank robbers rampaging in Twin Springs just when he was about to pay off his debts. With a clean slate he was going to ask Kathy to marry him. He reckoned now that he would have to give up such thoughts for a few years, and he had little hope of combating Dillon's challenge for so long.

He cast a savage glance at Dillon's handsome face, now comported into the right amount of concern and sorrow. The Bar Q man's eyes held his briefly and the mockery in them made Matt squirm. One thing seemed fairly evident to Matt, Dillon would not press home the fight whilst Kathy was around, wishing to appear the magnanimous, successful cattle rancher above petty range squabbles, and that mere fact influenced Matt to decide upon an immediate return to the Triple Bar after the funeral. He would never bring himself to hide behind a woman.

The service ended and Kathy walked to the edge of her father's grave. She checked the flow of tears as she looked down, then with her shoulders squared she turned away. Dillon and Nugent turned to follow her and their eyes met in mutual hate as they fell into step. The rest of the Bar Q men closed in behind them.

At the entrance to the Casino, the Bar Q

men stopped and stood alongside the horses they had left tethered to the hitch rail while Dillon and Matt continued up Main Street to the Rushland's house. Dillon paused for a moment and called out to one of his men, 'Go and find Jarman, Slim,' and when the puncher nodded, he caught up with the other two.

Outside her house Kathy turned impulsively to the two men.

'Now Lew, and you Matt, let this fighting stop. When the bank's affairs are settled we'll be repaying what we held in safe keeping for Matt, and I guess you can settle things then.'

Dillon shrugged his wide shoulders.

'I'll wait,' he said. 'But I reckon you can bypass Nugent with the dinero. He'll be in the hoosegow.'

'Howso?' Matt glared at the Bar Q man and Kathy's hand crept nervously to her mouth.

'I'll leave Jarman to tell you that. The law's his business.' Dillon's eyes were mocking. 'I'll mebbe use my influence so's you won't get your neck stretched.'

'Why – what's he supposed to have done?' There was a wild look in Kathy's eyes as she asked the question and Matt Nugent felt a sudden surge of elation at her concern for him.

'You'll hear all about it in good time,

Kathy,' Lew Dillon growled, turning on his heels. 'But mebbe Nugent would like to tell you first.'

The tall rancher walked swiftly back towards his waiting men and Jarman, who had just joined them with the puncher Slim.

'What's it all about, Matt?' Kathy asked, her eyebrows puckered with worry.

Nugent placed his hand on her arm encouragingly.

'Don't worry yourself, Kathy,' he said with a smile. 'Dillon thinks he's worked up some evidence against me for rustling his beef but he's plumb outa luck. The Texan, Bellamy, saw the evidence being faked and cleared the sign away after Dillon's men pulled out.'

The girl did not understand, but seeing that Nugent was not unduly perturbed she calmed and stepped up on to the veranda.

'You won't make anything of it, Matt?' she pleaded. 'Don't be driven to fighting. The odds are too great.'

Matt shook his head. 'Nobody's gonna railroad me into a gun battle unless the chances are fairly even. But with Clint Bellamy an' Mex Juarez siding me, the odds are thinning down some.' As he spoke he had one eye on Jarman who had detached himself from the crowd of Bar Q men and was walking purposefully up the street. 'You'd best get indoors Kathy. With Jarman around to see fair play there'll be no promiscuous lead throwing so you've got no call to worry.'

The girl studied Nugent's good-looking face anxiously and felt a depth of tenderness well up for him. It became apparent to her that to save his life she would be prepared for what would be the ultimate sacrifice, to marry Lew Dillon. She rested her hand on his arm briefly and went indoors, but she was at the window watching when Jarman stopped a few yards away from Nugent. Her feathery touch sent the blood running fast in Matt Nugent's veins and he turned to eye Jarman without rancour.

'You'd better get your cayuse Nugent,' Jarman said. 'Dillon reckons he's got the deadwoods on you for rustling his stock.'

Matt said nothing and Jarman swallowed heavily.

'I'm not taking his sayso,' he continued. 'I've told him we'll all ride along to see the evidence. If you're in the clear you've got nothing to worry about.'

Nugent shrugged his slim shoulders and stepped down from the sidewalk.

'C'mon, let's go,' he growled.

A few minutes later they rode out of town, Nugent sandwiched between Jarman and Lew Dillon with hard-faced Bar Q crew in close attendance.

'Here they come.'

Mex nodded towards the distant dust

113

cloud that slowed just clear of the shimmering heat haze, and Clint Bellamy shaded his eyes, squinting in the direction indicated.

'Yeah, seems to be enough of 'em too. I reckon Dillon's gonna be a mite upset when he finds he can't hang Nugent all nice an' legal.'

The pards shifted their positions and relaxed with a smoke while the dust cloud crept closer. They were lying between two boulders perched on the northern rim of the dry wash. Their horses stood just below them, ground hitched and cropping the short bunch grass desultorily.

'They're heading this way sure enough Mex. D'you reckon they've got Jarman and Nugent along?'

'Sure thing, an' it's my bet Dillon's gonna be meaner than a fresh-branded brush steer.'

A few minutes sufficed to prove the Mexican right. They were able to pick out Nugent riding between Jarman and Dillon with the rest of the Bar Q men packed close behind them. Quickly the riders approached the dry wash, the hoofbeats sounding like the rising roll of thunder. Briefly they were lost to sight when they passed behind a fold that led to the entrance of the wash and at that moment the pards ran swiftly down to their mounts and swung into their saddles. They rode up the grade and reined in at the top. Each held a gun at the ready.

The riders below hauled their sweating horses to a halt. All eyes were rivetted to the shale floor, searching for the evidence that was to seal Nugent's fate. There was a sardonic grin on Nugent's dust-grimed face while Dillon's lips were parted in a grimace of savagery. A few of the crew appeared more than a little perplexed. Jarman rubbed a horny palm over his sweating face.

'This the place, Dillon?' he growled, and Dillon jerked his head round to survey a group of his men. One of them nodded and shrugged his shoulders as if disassociating himself from the whole business.

'Yeah, this is the place all right,' Dillon shouted. 'Seems they've cleared up the evidence but that don't alter the facts. I reckon if we follow the sign outa this wash, we'll come up with the steers Nugent stole.'

Disbelief showed on Jarman's face and he shook his head.

'I'm not taking Nugent in on your sayso, Dillon,' he said. 'If I come up with any proof he'll have to take his chances with a jury but I want proof; solid proof.'

'You durned old goat,' yelled Dillon. 'You just keep a watch on Nugent. I'll soon round up the proof you want with some of my crew.'

'You stay right there, Dillon!'

Clint's voice was clear and authoritative and all eyes were turned up to where the pards sat their mounts with quiet calm. A man made a move behind Dillon and Mex fired once. The man's scream died in his throat and a couple of horses reared when he pitched out of the saddle.

The Bar Q men froze as Clint and Mex coaxed their mounts gently down the steep grade. There was a certain something about the set of the pards' features that proclaimed they were now playing for keeps. Dillon's hands stayed well away from his guns but he glared at Jarman murderously.

'What're you waiting for, Jarman?' he shouted. 'You're so allfired set on doing your duty right. Ain't you gonna blast these murdering bank robbers now you've got the chance?'

The lawman blew out his cheeks with exasperation as he realized just how far he was being alienated from the most powerful rancher in his territory, but he was bolstered with the knowledge that his close friendship with Don Lear would still bring in its percentage from the Bar Q, so he stood his ground. He shook his head.

'You're plumb outa luck, Dillon,' Mex grated. 'Jarman's got himself wised up about my pard an' me, an' that leaves us in the clear, which is more than can be said for you hombres.'

Dillon's face was a study until he brought himself under control. Behind him horses were fidgeting and some of his men were counting the chances of going for their hardware. Collectively it was certain that gunplay would give the Bar Q inevitable victory, but individually chances of survival were too uncertain to risk setting the battle in motion. The men relaxed and left things to Dillon. He was too wise a bird to be pushed into premature action with the law looking on, and he changed his tack.

'That right you've cleared 'em, Jarman?'

Jarman nodded. While the talking went on Matt Nugent gigged his mount away from the ruck of riders and taking out a gun he turned to level the weapon at Dillon. When he spoke his words were directed to Jarman.

'When I set out with you from town I knew just what you would find here. Bellamy saw Bar Q men working on their own steers with a running iron yesterday, an' herding them into this wash. He headed 'em right back on Dillon's territory an' that's where they are right now. Looks like he's mighty keen to get me set up for a necktie party.'

The look that Dillon gave Clint was one of utter hate but the Texan grinned back at him unabashed.

'Want me to tell you who did the faking?' Clint asked. 'They're all there right behind you. The four hombres huddled close to that spavined squint-eyed bustard.'

The squint-eyed puncher went deep purple with rage and he had to hold on fiercely to his saddle pommel to restrain himself going for his guns. Dillon made no attempt to follow the direction indicated by Clint. He just turned away to give Jarman a straight look.

'All right Jarman, if you want to take Nugent's sayso, I reckon that's your funeral. Just mark this well. I'll give him two days to pull out of the Triple Bar an' you'd better see he goes or else any more blood spilt on this range will be your responsibility. The Triple Bar already belongs to me and I'm giving due warning that trespassers will be shot.'

'Why wait two days,' Clint put in before Jarman could speak. 'What's wrong with now?' the Texan's face was set hard and his pard's grin widened as Dillon eyed their guns.

'The only thing wrong with now is that you've got the drop. I reckon we can wait.'

Clint nodded. 'That being so, just unhitch those gunbelts an' let 'em drop. Any man getting itchy fingers bites the dust.'

Time seemed to hang still while the Bar Q men watched Lew Dillon, waiting for his next move. The tension eased away and one after another they unhitched their gunbelts, following Dillon's lead. He waved his men away and after picking up the wounded man, they set their mounts into action, heading out of the wash towards the Bar Q. Dillon stayed to let his brittle gaze rest on the four men in turn.

'Don't get carried away by what's just happened,' he said. 'Right from now I'm giving instructions to my crew to shoot on sight. Like I said, we'll keep to our own range for the next two days then we're moving in.'

Nugent went to speak but Mex motioned him to silence.

'Two days will be plenty for us, Dillon,' Mex said. 'I reckon we'll have the answers to that bank robbery by then and Nugent'll have his dinero back.'

The Bar Q boss was visibly shaken by the Mexican's remark. There was a thoughtful expression on his face when he hauled his spirited bay gelding around and touched the animal with his spurs.

'What did you mean about getting the answers to the bank robbery?' Jarman asked as Dillon disappeared round the bend at the head of the dry wash. 'You been keeping information to yourself?'

Mex shook his head. 'Nope, but it won't hurt any to let the news get around that the trail is hot.'

Jarman looked unimpressed. He slid out of the saddle and started to gather the gunbelts. Nugent and the pards watched him incuriously. For the second time the marshal staggered back to his cayuse with an armful of belts and fastened them wherever he could. He rested briefly with one hand on the saddle cantle.

119

'It's my guess Dillon's got you over a barrel, Nugent,' he said. 'An' I'm thinking I've gone as far as I can to hold him off. If you take my advice you'll move out like he says. If you stay, the way I see it, he's got every cause to start throwing lead.'

Jarman climbed back into the saddle and started to head his horse towards the Bar Q.

'You say you can't hold Dillon off any longer, Jarman?' Clint called after him.

The marshal turned in the saddle and nodded.

'Then I reckon you'd better swear in a couple of deputies.'

'Yah, like who?' Jarman snorted.

'My pard an' me. That'll make it nice an' legal if we've gotta twist Dillon's tail some in tracking down the bank robbers, an' give us some status if we take a hand in stopping a range war developing.'

'Considering you're both lined up with Nugent it would sure look as if I was taking sides.' Jarman spat out the words. 'I ain't so sure I'd pick Nugent if it came to taking sides.'

'You're durned right,' Nugent replied. 'If Bellamy and Juarez hadn't turned up here I reckon you'd have shown what side you favoured. Well I'm not moving on, and if Dillon wants the Triple Bar he'll have to burn a lot of powder.'

Jarman's face went expressionless and he

shrugged his broad shoulders. He went to gig his mount then paused and rested his eyes on Clint.

'Howcome you say twist Dillon's tail in tracking down the bank robbers?'

'Because the robbery was planned on Bar Q territory,' Clint asserted. 'That sourdough who spread the gold strike news headed straight for Bar Q range off the Rawlins trail and met up with a war party of Bar Q waddies. They killed the burro and left it for buzzard meat.'

'Huh, that don't mean a thing Bellamy,' Jarman snorted. 'There's an awful lot of Dillon range and because the bank robbers headed out from there it don't follow that Dillon is involved.'

Clint shrugged and eyed the gunbelts significantly. 'Mebbe when you've finished the chore you've set yourself you'll get to doing some tracking,' he replied. 'Could be you'll get to finding the answers on your lonesome.'

Jarman grunted and headed his horse out of the wash towards the Bar Q.

'You fellers have sure got Jarman in a dither,' Nugent said when the marshal was lost to view around the bend. 'He wants to side with Dillon, that's where his bread is buttered, but he's not so sure now that Dillon's going to be left holding all the aces.'

The pards grinned and hauled their horses around.

121

'We'd better get out of this wash,' Mex reminded Nugent. 'I shouldn't think the Bar Q men will have gone far and when Jarman hands 'em back their shooting irons they might try to take the initiative.'

Nugent saw the point and they all rode off in the opposite direction to that taken by the Bar Q men and Jarman.

'Y'know Nugent,' Clint said when they had made a few miles towards the Triple Bar headquarters. 'In your place I'd move out like Dillon says.'

Matt Nugent slewed in the saddle to stare at Clint but the Texan was quite serious.

'I'm thinking we'll do more good working from town than from the Triple Bar where we'll be stretched to the limit checking on Dillon's moves.'

Nugent chewed the suggestion over for a bit then turned towards Mex for his opinion.

'That's hoss sense to me,' Mex agreed. 'But it's up to you, Nugent. If you want to make a stand at the Triple Bar then I guess it's all right by us.'

They rode in silence for a long time while Nugent came to terms with himself. He realized he had no right to expect these two men to make a stand for the Triple Bar at the ranch house against their better judgment. It was natural for him to think of defending his headquarters and took a deep breath before announcing his decision.

'We'll get the rest of those brush steers branded and driven back into the brush and then I guess we'll head for town like you say.'

Clint and Mex exchanged satisfied glances but made no comment.

Lew Dillon's face was dark with anger as he rode out of the dry wash. Bellamy and Juarez were beginning to get into his hair. Right from their first meeting in Twin Springs he had felt a vague sense of unease about them and as time and again they showed up to thwart his plans, this had grown into a positive belief that unless he could bring about their early demise, they would help Nugent to keep the Triple Bar out of his grasp.

His men were waiting for him, all grouped on the skyline a mile away, but his attention was taken by the lone rider making fast time on the trail cut by the party to the dry wash. His lip curled as he recognized Kathleen Rushland and he hauled his mount savagely to a halt as he reasoned her haste was occasioned by concern for Matt Nugent. He had to struggle to get his expression adjusted before the girl rode up to him. The dust lay thick on her white mare and the steam rose up from the animal's flanks in an acrid cloud.

'What happened, Lew?' There was deep anxiety in the girl's voice. 'Where's Matt?'

Dillon waved an arm towards the head of

the wash. 'Nothing's happened,' he growled. 'Nugent's down there with his sidekicks.'

Relief flooded Kathy's face. 'I – I just couldn't stay in town,' she stammered. 'You two are so headstrong. I was afraid that something would happen that would only cause misery and regret.'

She went to guide her mare's head towards the dry wash when the control snapped in Dillon's string-taut mind. He leaned over and caught hold of her reins. The fire in his eyes acted as a shock to her sensitive system when she looked up at him.

'Your concern for Nugent is out of proportion to his worth,' he snapped. 'Why in heck do women always have to rush to protect the shiftless hombres who can't keep a spread on its uppers?'

'If Matt is given a chance he'll get the Triple Bar back on its feet,' Kathy replied with some heat.

'Well, there's only one thing that's gonna give him a chance.' Dillon spoke slowly and his eyes bored into the girl's with grim intent. 'I'll lay off him on condition you get yourself nicely hitched up as Mrs Dillon within the week.'

The hasty refusal that rose to the girl's tongue died away before it was uttered. She looked with mute dismay into the man's relentless eyes and her senses swam as his overpowering desire flowed into her. She pulled herself together with an effort.

'I don't think this is the time or place for wedding talk, Lew.' Her voice was unsteady but she said her piece. 'And I would sure hate to marry anyone on account of a threat.'

'Huh, you'd pretty soon forget the reasons for marrying me, Kathy.' Dillon's laugh was brittle. 'You'd enjoy it fine. I reckon I'm enough of a man to chase all other thoughts out of your head.'

The colour mounted Kathy's face as the thought fleeted through her mind that Dillon certainly was virile enough to satisfy what most women wanted in a man.

'So it's up to you,' Dillon continued. 'You can ride on down there and side with Nugent, and I'll run him off that spread so fast he won't stop this side of Montana, that's if he lives, or you can head for town and get fixed up for a wedding. That way I'll leave Nugent alone. I guess he'll run himself outa business soon enough anyway.'

Even as he spoke his active mind was busy with ways of despatching Nugent without any possibility of blame being attached to him. His reasons for wanting the Triple Bar were more pressing than the girl could ever guess and his words to her meant nothing to him. In point of fact Katy Rushland's too evident concern for Nugent made it urgent for Dillon not only to take over the man's spread but to ensure also his early death.

Kathy bit her lip, her mind a mad whirl of thought. One thing she grasped at in despair; the element of time. Dillon had said a wedding within a week. If she rode down to join Nugent than his chances would be gone but a week might see a change in the situation. The memory of the two enigmatical men who were siding Nugent flashed through her mind. She pictured the young stocky Texan with the shrewd eyes and calm mien, and the handsome sardonic Mexican; yes, with those men helping, a week could make a difference. She straightened in the saddle and gave Dillon look for look than she nodded slowly.

'I guess I'll ride into town,' she said.

Dillon grinned and the temper went out of him, bringing back the charm in his well-moulded face. He released her reins and pulled his mount aside so that she could turn her mare round.

'That's good sense, Kathy,' he said quietly. 'I guess you and I are gonna get along fine.'

Her smile was one of relief but Dillon took it as sign of final acceptance. As the girl turned her mount and headed for town, he watched her go in fine good humour. His eyes lingered on her shapely form until the dust hid it from view and he stayed immobile for minutes afterwards, letting his senses run on ahead of time.

CHAPTER SEVEN

'Waal, I guess that takes care of those critturs,' Nugent grunted, wiping his streaming face with his bandana. 'Hardly seems worth having dug 'em out.'

Clint and Mex wiped their own faces and grinned sympathetically at the Triple Bar man.

'They carry your brand now,' Clint reminded him but Nugent's brow was creased in a frown.

'Yeah, my brand's on 'em right enough but the only trouble is, I'll have no range to graze 'em on the next time the critturs see daylight.'

It was natural that Nugent should view the future with misgivings and neither Clint nor Mex were inclined to fill him with false hopes. They had branded the rest of the brush steers and herded them across the northern range to the chapparal and sage brush. On the way they collected another fifty head and now every last one was deep in the brush. Dyer, Rinty Denver and Con Levis rode out of the brush and hauled their mounts to a stop. The youngsters searched for the makings whilst Dyer took a sizable bite out of thick plug of tobacco. They looked to Nugent for the next move.

'I reckon we'd better head for town.'

There was no enthusiasm in Nugent's voice but his remark brought a look of relief to the faces of Denver and Levis. Dyer's square face showed no particular interest but he kept his gaze well away from Clint Bellamy.

Dyer was surprised the Texan had made no announcement that Dillon's note had been taken from him during his sleep, and although there was no apparent reason for Bellamy to suspect Dyer, the man felt vaguely uncomfortable each time Clint's shrewd eyes rested on him. The way the two pardners kept their own counsel was having an unnerving effect on Nugent's segundo, and the longer he stayed in their company the longer their shadows seemed to stretch.

'I guess I'll collect that second string cayuse of mine then.' Dyer tried to make his tone conversational. 'I've gotta buyer for him in Rawlins.'

Nugent gave him a quick glance of annoyance which faded as quickly. The way that Dyer was discounting the possibility of requiring his second-string horse on the Triple Bar angered Nugent temporarily, but he had to admit the common sense that prompted Dyer's decision. He nodded and turned towards Denver and Levis.

'We'll take the other spare cayuses into town,' he said. 'I guess there'll be room for 'em in that corral of Rushland's.'

The two young men stubbed out their cigarettes and pulled their horses around without further ado. Dyer missed out Clint when he made his perfunctory farewell and followed in the wake of the two youngsters.

'You coming?' Nugent asked the pards.

'Nope. I guess we'll join you later,' Mex said. 'There's a whole lot of this territory we haven't checked on an' now seems a good time to see some more of it.'

'See you in town then,' Nugent replied, and as the pards raised their hands in farewell, he rode away.

The two watched him join up with his crew and appear over the rim of a fold, then together they set off to skirt the brush and hug the hills that bordered the Triple Bar.

The foothills ranging the Triple Bar did not run much to a pattern. Some rose smoothly at a steady gradient out of the prairie bunch grass to nicely-moulded summits, while others were stark, ragged, rocky outcrops, rising steeply in unscaleable walls to pointed peaks. The latter were serried with ravines, gullies and cul-de-sacs. To make a detailed survey of the hills the pardners would have needed a couple of weeks, so they contented themselves with memorizing the main details while pushing on to Bar Q range.

Mex pulled his pinto to a stop as they rounded the shoulder of one of the more accessible hills. He pointed to a moving horseman below who had a riderless horse towing along.

'That's Dyer. He's sure some way off track if he's headed for Rawlins.'

Clint grinned at him. 'I reckon he knows where he's heading, and I'm plumb curious to know where that is.'

'Yeah, a deep hombre is Dyer,' commented Mex. 'It's my bet he knows a lot more of what's going on hereabouts than Nugent would ever credit.'

The two men relapsed into silence and set about stalking their man. For a few miles they kept to the shoulder of the hills, then when they came to a sheer wall they headed down on to the plain and allowed Dyer plenty of elbow room.

'He's bypassing Dillon's headquarters,' Mex muttered a few miles later. 'He'd have turned south-east by now if he'd been making for the ranch house.'

Now and again they caught sight of Dyer, riding hunched up in the saddle, but for the most part they were content to let him keep well ahead with Mex following his trail without apparent effort. They forded the river at the point where it dropped to the plain out of the hillside and picked up the trail on the other side. For another hour they followed

Dyer, now hugging the line of hills, until at length his trail entered a cut in the mountains.

The pards dismounted and fitted muffles to the hooves of their mounts before following into the cut, and from the moment the walls of the cut shut out most of the daylight from them they moved forward with care and watchfulness.

It was apparent to them that efforts had been made to remove sign at the entrance, because as they progressed deeper into the mountain they saw evidence of large scale cattle movement through the cut and of many shod horses. They rode with ears and eyes attuned to pick up any suspicious move or noise. Each man had one hand on the butt of his gun, ready to trade lead on split second notice.

For all of an hour they continued along the eerie twisting route, the rock walls at all times nearly blocking out the sunlight, until they came to a blank rock face that barred further progress. Strewn at the foot of the dead end wall were a number of large boulders, all big enough to hide a couple of riders and these they approached with due care, but no one lay in wait for them. They dismounted, and hiding their horses behind one of the boulders, examined the cliff face with minute care.

Mex shrugged his shoulders and turning

away from the end wall, retraced his steps, his sharp eyes scouring the rock floor for sign. What he sought was easy enough to find. Cattle and men just do not vanish into thin air. Clint was right behind him when the hiss of satisfaction escaped from the Mexican's smiling lips. The Texan leaned forward to follow the direction of his pard's pointing finger. Where it appeared as though the cut widened abruptly, an opening ran back parallel to the cut for some way. It was wide enough for about four steers to pass abreast.

'Better leave the cayuses where they are until we know where this leads,' whispered Clint.

Mex nodded and they moved into the opening as silently as Comanches. After running straight for about a hundred yards, the cut turned abruptly to the right and ran upwards at a steady gradient. For half a mile or so they climbed until they came to a sharp turn to the left. At this point the two men were even more cautious and, at a sign from Mex, Clint froze into watchfulness whilst the Mexican inched quietly forward. A couple of minutes later Mex was back, waving for Clint to join him.

They climbed together to the point where the cut started to descend and Mex pulled Clint forward to a vantage point that gave a minute view of a scene stretched some way below them. The cut opened out on to a grass valley, almost hidden from view by vast concave basalt cliff walls. Just a long thin stretch of the valley was visible to them but there was enough cattle in that stretch to convince them a fair-sized herd grazed below.

'More than one brand amongst that lot, Clint,' whispered Mex.

'Yeah, I can make out Triple Bar, Bar Q and Lazy K. Looks as though some hombres are outsmarting Dillon as well on this range.'

'Could be just a blind having his own steers mixed up with rustled stock,' Mex muttered. 'Considering all this leads off his range he'd be a durned fool not to make it look as though he was suffering along with the other spreads.'

'Look!' Mex pointed again to where the valley below curved away from view. Clint saw the two riders just before the towering rock wall hid them from sight.

'Huh-huh, Lear and Dyer. Heading back this way.' Clint took a quick look round. 'They'll be here in ten minutes at the most. Reckon we've got cover enough?'

'Yeah, if we stay right here I'm thinking they'll pass without seeing us, that's unless they've got mighty spooky cayuses.'

Just a couple of foot-high boulders lay between the pards and the rocky trail but the riders would be coming up out of a sunlit valley into the gloom of the cut and should be passing the pards at the moment when their eyes were least adjusted to the change in light.

The pardners made themselves comfortable but took the precaution of drawing their guns in readiness. Neither man had any qualms about facing Dyer or Lear but this was not the place nor time. Nearly ten minutes went by before the rhythmic hoofbeats first became audible and a further couple of minutes before Dyer and Lear came abreast of them. Clint and Mex both held their breath but there was no need for exaggerated caution. The two rustlers were engrossed in their own business.

'Always pays to let a man think he's king,' Lear was saying. 'Gets so stiff-necked he can't see what's under his nose.'

Dyer's laugh echoed along the walls of the cut. 'When we move out this time we can head straight east. We'll...'

Dyer's reply tailed away leaving the pards mystified as to what Lear and Dyer intended doing some place east, but the words implied the two men had worked together before hitting the Twin Springs-Rawlins range.

Clint and Mex waited until the riders had passed well out of earshot, then scrambling to their feet they made their way back down the long cut to where their horses nodded and dozed.

'Could be a coupla hundred head of Triple Bar steers in that valley,' Clint remarked as he rolled himself a cigarette. 'Looks like Dyer an' Lear have been building a herd over a long time. Nugent's stock is sure run down some now on account of the trail herd he sold and I guess he'd have known if he'd been left with that number after the round-up so it follows they'd been rustled before he collected the trail herd together.'

Mex drew hard on the cheroot he had lit until it was going to his satisfaction, then he climbed into the saddle.

'That's the way I figure it too,' he said. 'An' that means the critturs are safe where they are until Lear and Dyer move out, so there's no call for us to get all steamed up cutting out Triple Bar beef an' herding 'em on to Nugent's range. We'd have to drive 'em into the brush anyways.'

'I guess we know now why Dillon hasn't made any more play with that note held on the Triple Bar,' Clint remarked as he climbed astride his gelding. 'When I followed Dyer on to Bar Q range I reckoned he'd gone to hand the note back to Dillon. It's my bet Lear's holding it now.'

The pards gigged their mounts into action and rode slowly back the way they had come, down the long gloomy cut and into the scorching heat of the late afternoon sun. Both men were busy with their thoughts and both arrived at the same conclusion; that Lear seemed to be holding a lot of good cards. He appeared set to gain no matter who else fell by the wayside. Without the evidence of the note, Dillon could come to grief with the law for taking the Triple Bar by force but Lear could slide out from under as being an employee acting in good faith under the impression his employer had legal right.

It was late afternoon when Nugent, Levis and Denver rode into Twin Springs. At the big corral on the edge of town where old man Rushland had grazed his prized sorrels, Levis and Denver stopped with the half dozen horses they had collected from the Triple Bar while Nugent went on in to see Kathy. He got no response from the house so he rode on up Main Street to the bank.

Leaving his horse at the hitchrail he climbed to the sidewalk and pushed the stout door open. Kathy's blonde hair showed above the tall back of a desk inside the room, and opening the hinged counter he walked through to her side. The girl looked up from the ledger she had been studying. The smile of welcome that flooded to her eyes and lips faded as quickly, and the troubled look that took its place shocked Nugent.

He knew that the girl's affection for her father had been very real and that everything would be tinged with sorrow for her for some considerable time, but Kathy's haggard drawn look and worried eyes drew hard on his sympathy.

'Wh-what do you want Matt?' she asked, pushing her chair away and standing up.

He took a step towards her but she backed away, her hand to her face.

'I've just brought my remuda into town, Kathy,' he replied, his manner becoming stiff. 'Thought you might let me keep 'em in that corral of yours.'

The girl nodded, her eyes downcast.

'Yes, of course Matt, help yourself.' She raised her eyes briefly and he saw that there was a light relief in them when she continued: 'So you're going to stay in town?'

'Yeah, for the time being.' Matt's face was bleak now. 'I guess things will work themselves out.'

'I hope so Matt and without any more bloodshed too.'

The misery was back in the girl's face and Matt sensed that she wanted him to leave. There was so much he wanted to say to her, and so much he wanted to hear from her, but her manner was building up a wall of reserve. He twirled his sombrero in his fingers a few times, indecision on his handsome face, then he half turned.

'Thanks then, Kathy. I don't know how long my broncs will be eating your graze but I'm sure glad to save the livery bill.'

When the girl did not reply, he continued his turn and made his way back through the hinged counter flap.

'Matt!'

He swung round at the door when the girl called to him, his heart pounding. Kathy had stepped some considerable way forward but she stopped when he turned, and whatever she wanted to say she stifled back. Nugent waited while she battled with herself but when it was apparent she had changed her mind, he hurried out to the sidewalk, his lips set in a hard line.

Riding back to the Rushland's pasture he watched Denver and Levis turn his spare horses loose, then the three of them rode to the livery stable together where they left their regular mounts. They took time out after to a get a bath and a meal at Seth Harben's gimcrack hotel, before getting the feel of the town.

Seth Harben was at the door watching the stage for Rawlins get under way when Nugent and his men re-emerged.

'I didn't get to hearing much about that gold strike on Seminoe Peak,' Nugent said. 'What did you make of it Seth?'

Harben ran his hand through his sparse hair and looked shame-faced.

'Don't reckon you will hear much about it, Matt,' he replied with a shrug. 'I guess we're all pretty sore at having high-tailed out on the sayso of an old coot of a sourdough, especially now we know we left the town so thin that poor old Dan Rushland an' Cressy didn't stand a chance.'

'Can't blame yourself, Seth,' Nugent said consolingly. 'I reckon gold's a mighty powerful word wherever it's spoken.'

Old Rube yelled and cracked his whip over the heads of his team and the Rawlins stage moved out, sending the dust billowing up. Nugent gave the dust time to resettle before nodding to Harben and making his way along the sidewalk. Denver and Levis followed him, eager to sample any delights that town might offer.

When they drew alongside the Casino, they paused and looked down Main Street to where half a dozen riders came in off the southern trail. Dillon's tall figure astride the big bay gelding was unmistakable. The other men were the hard-case ruffians who usually travelled in close attendance. Nugent stiffened as the riders bore down upon them and the two youngsters licked their lips involuntarily as a wave of apprehension touched them. When Dillon pulled his mount to a halt just a few yards away, the Triple Bar men were in command of themselves, and despite the odds were ready to take things as they came.

Dillon's men fanned out, eyes bright, expectant; these were the odds they liked. Dillon's face was mocking. Seeing Nugent and his remaining crew in town spelt surrender to him, and with victory now in his grasp he despised the Triple Bar man for not making a stand. His lips parted in a sneering smile but he said nothing. Jarman came out of his office, taking in the scene, but Dillon ignored him. Having promised Kathy Rushland not to force Nugent's hand, Dillon was keeping hold of his tongue, but he hoped to bring the Triple Bar man into action without words.

As Nugent stared back at him with rapidly rising temper it looked as though Dillon would get his way, but the bank door opened and Kathy Rushland appeared to appraise the situation quickly. Her heart gave a twist of fear as she saw the decision take hold of Matt Nugent. All along the sidewalk on both sides of the dusty road men leaned, watching intently. The air was charged with tension and the folk of Twin Springs were drawn like vultures sensing a feast.

'Lew! Lew!'

The girl's voice rang out sharp and clear, and every head turned to watch her rush from the bank on to the road to where Dillon's gelding stood as though carved in stone.

The colour ebbed away from Nugent's

140

face as he watched the girl place her hand on Dillon's knee and turn her face up to the Bar Q men to talk in a low voice. The tension drained away from him to be replaced by an utter weariness. He hardly noticed the wide grins of Dillon's men. He felt sick and nothing seemed to matter any more. He saw Dillon lean over and place a hand placatingly on Kathy's shoulder then he turned abruptly, almost pushing Denver and Levis aside as he thrust his way into the Casino. He missed the look of agony that Kathy Rushland flashed in his direction as he disappeared through the batwing doors.

Normally of moderate drinking habits, he started in to punish the harsh rye that Joe Mears kept handing out. Con Levis and Rinty Denver took up positions each side of him and drank sparingly. They saw Dillon's men crowd into the saloon and were prepared to die desperately if necessary, but Dillon must have given strict instructions to his roughneck crew to lay off. The Bar Q men ignored them. They settled around a table and after getting in the drinks, started a game of poker.

Later on Dillon came into the saloon in company with Jarman. Neither man took any notice of Nugent as they came up to the bar but Jarman planted himself solidly between the two men in an attempt to prevent contact. Nugent turned and glared at the marshal.

'Howcome you've got time to belly up drinkin'?' he growled. 'You found the bustards who rubbed out Rushland?'

Jarman coloured but fought down the hasty reply that came to his lips. He shrugged his shoulders and turned his attention to Mears, the bartender, who was busy pouring the drinks out of Dillon's bottle. Now that things were going his way, Dillon was magnanimously ignoring Jarman's previous defection and the marshal seemed eager enough to bury the hatchet.

'D'you hear what I say Jarman?' Nugent insisted, and the lawman turned, a nasty light in his eyes.

'Yeah, I heard you Nugent,' he growled. 'An' I'm keeping my eyes skinned. Sooner or later somebody's gonna come into town with a fist full of dinero an' mebbe then I'll get a lead but I ain't gonna do any good forking my cayuse all over the territory. That way all I'll get is callouses.'

'Might get more sense in one of those callouses than you've got in your head,' Rinty Denver's quiet voice put in and Jarman glared at the youngster.

'You keep that lip buttoned Denver or by heck I'll tear your innards out.'

Denver looked unabashed and turned to his drink while Nugent gave it up, eyeing his empty glass with indecision. He made his mind up and pushed it across the counter for a refill.

A couple of hours slipped by with the Casino filling up and the uneasy atmosphere mounting to one of charged tension. Nugent was well into his second bottle and his two young sidekicks had already taken more drink than they were accustomed to carry. Whereas Nugent was now only interested in the drink, Denver and Levis were eyeing Dillon and his men seated at the table with brash insolence. The townsfolk, who knew enough of the circumstances, kept respectful distance but stayed on so that they might not miss anything that could erupt.

Two more men came through the batwing doors, Lear and Dyer. They paused for a moment, taking in the situation, then when Lear carried on up to the bar to join Dillon, it was significant that Dyer chose a table as far away from his old boss Nugent as possible.

Lear took the drink Dillon proffered, and tossing it down in one gulp gazed around the room. His glance came to rest on the two young Triple Bar men who gave him look for look. Lear's temper started to rise as sneering grins appeared on the faces of the two youngsters. He stepped away from the bar and took a deep breath.

'You hombres got anything to say?' he questioned with a snarl.

143

'Yeah, you're a rustlin' coyote,' Denver said without batting an eyelid.

'And you never had a pa,' put in Levis for good measure.

They both came away from the bar as they spoke but they both staggered under the influence of the spirit they had consumed. Nearly all eyes were focused on the speakers. Dillon made to say something to Lear then changed his mind. Jarman ignored the proceedings and kept his eyes glued over the bar. Nugent stirred out of his misery, suddenly aware that his men were getting into something deep. He made to straighten up and take a hand when the place erupted.

Denver and Levis went for their guns and Lear slipped smoothly into action. The explosions coincided with the thud as Daniels, the Casino owner, brought a bottle down on Nugent's head. Neither Denver nor Levis stood a chance. They both pitched to the sawdust floor with their guns only half drawn, and Nugent fell in a heap on top of them. Lear stood, his face an evil mask, a smoking gun in each hand, completely unconcerned.

'You saw the way of it,' he said at length to Jarman who had turned round at the moment of truth. 'You saw 'em go for their irons.'

'Sure thing, Don,' the marshal answered. 'They called the tune.'

There was a rush to examine Lear's handi-work and when the townsfolk pulled Nugent's unconscious form away, they found the two young punchers were both dead.

'Better get 'em to the funeral parlour,' said Jarman taking over. 'And a few of you had better take Nugent to the pokey. I guess he'll be better where I can see him for to-night.'

The group of men did as they were asked and after the two corpses had been taken away, Jarman followed the men who carried Nugent. A few townsfolk eyed Dyer curi-ously, wondering whether he would take up the Triple Bar's quarrel but that individual remained impassive and aloof, and soon the tension relaxed.

CHAPTER EIGHT

The light had almost vanished when Bellamy and Juarez rode into Twin Springs. They hauled their mounts to a halt just as the Casino's batwing doors were flung open and the townsfolk spilled out carrying the dead men. Mex laid a restraining hand on the Texan's arm as his pard made to ride forward. Recognition of the corpses had been immediate.

'Won't do those any good now, Clint,' Mex said quietly but his face was hard.

They watched Nugent being carried out and both heaved sighs of relief to see he was only unconscious. Blood ran down the side of his face from the spot on his head the bottle had opened. They edged their mounts out of the way as Nugent was carried past to the gaol house. Jarman did not see them.

'We've gotta break this thing mighty soon, Mex,' Clint gritted. 'Or else Dillon's gonna win all along the line. Nugent's left right out on a limb now.'

They drew back further into the shadows, their minds active with the problems that were becoming more pressing every hour.

'Now's the time to start playing one against

147

the other,' Mex replied. 'I reckon we've got enough to get 'em looking over their shoulders.'

They dismounted and led their mounts between two buildings opposite the Casino then leaving them ground hitched, they mingled with the crowd of townsfolk who were excitedly recounting the gunplay some of them had been privileged to see. The death of two young punchers seemed not to concern any of these men, who slavered over a gunfight much as the madding crowd in a bull fight scream for the coup-de-grace. From the scraps of conversation the pardners were able to build up the picture of the events in the Casino.

'Might as well get these broncs stabled,' said Mex at length. 'I reckon we've got plenty to keep us in town for tonight.'

'Yeah, plenty,' Clint agreed.

They collected their horses and remounting, made their way to the livery stable. Shortly afterwards they took a hurried meal in the Chinese Chop House and went back out into the night to keep a watch on the comings and goings from the Casino. As the time dragged on the wind shifted, bringing the chill from the snow line, and the two men pulled their slickers around themselves and moved around a bit to keep the blood circulating. Possessed of unlimited patience and used to long weary vigils, they were prepared to wait all night if need be, but just after midnight the man they wanted was framed briefly in the light of the saloon as he pushed open the batwing doors.

Dyer stepped down from the sidewalk to where his mount stood nodding at the hitch-rail. He was about to untether the animal when Clint's gun stabbed into his back.

'You ain't goin' any place, Dyer,' Clint muttered. 'Just step along nice an' easy an' mebbe you'll live.'

Dyer stiffened with shock, then with Clint's gun prodding him walked slowly up Main Street. Only when they were beyond the livery stable was Clint satisfied.

'This'll do, Dyer,' he growled. Mex moved around the man, taking his guns out of his holsters, and tossing them into the grass verge.

'What in heck's got into you hombres?' Dyer said at last, finding his voice, but the Mexican's next compromising action took away his power of speech. Mex palmed his long bladed knife and held it so that the point pricked the skin underneath Dyer's chin.

'Plenty, you two-faced coyote.' The Mexican's quiet tones were chilling. 'We know that you're two-timing Nugent, an' that you an' Lear have it all planned to move out the herd of rustled cattle you've stached away in that hidden valley. So when we get to asking

149

questions you can cut out the lies. If we get the right answers then you'll take your chances with a jury. If we don't, I'll slit your throat.'

The man's quick intake of breath evidenced his surprise at the knowledge the pards had already gained. He did not doubt the Mexican would slit his throat without compunction and he checked the denial that flashed into his mind.

'Yeah, me an' Lear are in cahoots,' he whispered through clenched teeth. The point of the knife restricted easy speech.

'How about the bank robbery, an' killing old man Rushland and Cressy?' gritted Clint.

'No! No!' Dyer cried. 'I had no part in that.'

'And Lear?' the Texan persisted.

'I – I don't know. Honest to God I don't know.' The man swallowed carefully. 'Lear's pretty close,' he continued. 'He wouldn't be talking any if he'd had a hand in that.'

'Huh, I reckon we'll get him to talk soon enough,' growled Mex. 'And what about Dillon? Is he in with you and Lear with that herd you've stached away?'

'No, but he's thrown a pretty wide rope on this range an' we've only helped ourselves to a percentage, an' some of his own steers thrown in.'

'Reckon Dillon's gonna be cut up a mite when we tell him then,' Clint said with a short laugh. 'He's gonna say that he's lily-

150

white, and his own mavericks in that herd of yours is gonna prove him right. It's my bet he'll get you hanged just to keep his skin whole.'

Dyer had to call upon all his reserves of courage as his bleak future impressed itself upon him. Standing with the Texan's gun in his back, the Mexican's knife at his throat, and the wrath of Dillon still to come, the tremor that ran through his body was excusable.

Mex sheathed the knife and stepped away from the man.

'Now turn around and head for the hoosegow,' he said. 'We'll let Jarman look after you until we can get Lear and Dillon to hear what you've got to say.'

Dyer did as he was told, and with Clint's Colt sticking hard into his back he led the way back up Main Street.

Jarman gazed sourly at Nugent as the Triple Bar man groaned and raised his head from the straw-filled palliasse. The marshal was sitting on the bunk opposite Nugent.

'You're blamed lucky to be alive,' Jarman snarled. 'So quit groaning.'

Nugent shook his head a few times and the effects of the blow and the large quantity of spirit he had consumed went away quickly. He eyed Jarman with venom and rubbed his head tenderly.

'You do this?' he asked.

Jarman shook his head. 'Nope, Daniels hit you with a bottle. You were just gonna horn into a quarrel your sidekicks had picked with Lear. You're blamed lucky you ain't in the funeral parlour alongside Levis and Denver.'

A spasm of pain crossed Nugent's face and it was not occasioned by the twinge he felt at the seat of his injury. He was silent for a long time. He had liked both Levis and Denver a great deal and the fact they were dead did not bear thought. The added knowledge they were dead because they had seen fit to fight his battles did not help either.

'You had no call to hit the red-eye so's you couldn't keep a hold on them rannies,' Jarman went on stirring the wound inexorably. 'An' they had no reason to call the tune either. Dillon's crew were just busy celebrating the wedding in advance.' Jarman's eyes were bright as he watched Nugent for reaction.

'What wedding?' asked Nugent dully. Not that he had any doubts.

'Lew Dillon an' Kathy Rushland,' Jarman replied. 'They're planning on getting wed in a few days.'

Nugent dropped his head back on the palliasse and gazed hard-faced at the uncompromising ceiling. So that was it. He had been right earlier in the day. Kathy

Rushland's concern in trying to keep him from fighting it out with Dillon was purely on account of Dillon. Matt Nugent's lip curled in a grim sneer. So maybe all women were the same, he thought; all ready to throw in with the king-pin. In the midst of thoughts of vengeance, one fact wormed its way into his mind until at length he had to take hold of it and consider. Nothing would change his real love for Kathy Rushland, and her happiness was important to him; then if her happiness was bound with Dillon, out of consideration for Kathy he must forsake the fight for the Triple Bar.

The marshal stood up and stepped through the cell door. Nugent did not stir as the door slammed and Jarman turned the key quickly. He made his way out of the cell block and into his office. Instinctively he went to the cupboard in the corner and took out a new bottle of rye, but before he could sample the contents the street door was pushed open and Dyer preceded Clint Bellamy and Mex Juarez by a fraction. Jarman swung round in surprise. His glance took in Dyer's empty holsters and the grim expressions on the faces of the pardners.

'What in heck d'you want?' he demanded.

Clint propelled Dyer further into the room and backheeled the street door.

'Look after this hombre, Jarman,' he said. 'He's been playing a deep game with Lear, playing both ends against the middle. They've got 'emselves a fair-sized herd of rustled steers stached away in the mountains.'

Jarman's face was a study as he looked at the stocky Triple Bar foreman.

'Howcome you know that?' he asked.

'You can ask him while we go and find Dillon. I reckon he'll be all for stringing Dyer up when he knows they helped themselves out of rustled stock, and some of his own steers too.'

Jarman nodded, his eyes star bright. He motioned Dyer to a chair by the table but kept his mouth shut. In the time it took for Clint and Mex to reach the sidewalk he had reached a decision.

'We're gonna have to work fast to get you out of this mess,' he growled at Dyer who was visibly shaken by the turn of events. He nodded towards the bottle. 'Get yourself a drink while I turn Nugent loose out back.'

Dyer grasped the bottle like a drowning man at a straw. Jarman went through into the cell block, shutting the door behind him. Unlocking Nugent's cell he thrust the door open with a crash. Nugent swung his legs out of the bunk and stared up at him.

'C'mon,' the marshal grunted. 'I've got business elsewhere an' that means I want this place empty.'

The Triple Bar man got to his feet and

154

shrugged his shoulders. 'I can't recollect asking to come here in the first place, Jarman,' he replied. 'But I sure hate to keep you away from drinking with your cronies.'

The marshal's eyes narrowed but he said nothing. He went to the back door leading out of the cell block and drawing the double bolts that held it secure, thrust it open. He waited impatiently while Nugent gathered up his hat and slicker then when the Triple Bar man passed through out into the night he slammed the door shut, jammed the bolts back into place, locked up and went back into his office. Dyer was on his feet with a third of the contents of Jarman's bottle inside him but the marshal ignored him and reached for the bottle.

'Well – what's the next move?' The steadiness was back in Dyer's voice and he posed the question in confidence.

'I just got rid of Nugent,' replied Jarman easily. 'The less he knows about us the better. Just give him time to clear an' you can get away. My cayuse is out back saddled up. I reckon you know where to hole up until the heat's off an' we can move those steers out.'

Dyer had one ear cocked listening for footsteps along the sidewalk.

'Yeah, I know where to hole up right enough,' he replied. 'But we'll have to get that herd on the move mighty fast now that the blamed greaser and his pard knows about it.'

'They're just working on guesswork, an' planning for you to crack up when Dillon shows up,' Jarman retorted. 'Nothing's moved into that valley while they've been on this range an' it just ain't natural for them to have stumbled across it.' He shook his head decisively. 'Nope, it's just plain guesswork.'

Ten minutes went by with Dyer becoming edgy again, then the first sound of footsteps along the sidewalk brought him to his feet with a jump.

'They're coming.' He almost shouted the words.

There was a bitter smile on Jarman's face as he eyed the elderly Triple Bar foreman.

'You get going now.' Jarman was calm, unhurried. 'Through the cell block.'

Dyer was at the dividing door when Jarman called: 'You'll need this Jim.'

Dyer stopped and nodded when Jarman held one of his own guns by the barrel.

'Catch,' said Jarman, and threw the gun across the room.

Dyer's eyes were on the spinning gun and he failed to see the marshal's second weapon clear leather. He caught the butt end dexteriously in a firm grasp then staggered and fell as Jarman's other gun emptied, ploughing a bullet straight through his heart. The footsteps stopped outside the door and Jarman turned towards it, the smoke idling up from the barrel of his gun.

Clint and Mex pushed their way into the smoke-ladened Casino and eyed the occupants carefully. Most of Daniels' customers were too steeped in rotgut to take much interest in the newcomers but the group around Dillon at the bar turned and watched the pardners with grim concern. Lear's hand moved towards his gun but Dillon's hand stayed him. The pardners kept on coming down the long aisle between the tables; both of them had their thumbs hooked in their gunbelts. They stopped just in front of Dillon's crew and looked past the men to Mears, the barkeep.

'Rye,' Clint called out, and Dillon's men eased apart a little to allow Mears to pass the glasses. The pards tossed their drink down and turned their attention to Dillon.

'We've gotta hombre in the hoosegow who's ready to shoot his mouth off about the rustling on this range,' Clint said blandly. 'Seems the rustlers have been rustled,' he continued, noting the glint come into Lear's eyes. 'From what he's already told us we reckoned you'd like to hear him say his piece again, Dillon.'

The Bar Q man glared at the pards with open dislike but he was loth to push the quarrel with these two men. It seemed to him that Nugent was licked, and with Kathy

157

Rushland promised to him he doubted whether Bellamy and Juarez could affect his plans any more.

'Anybody I know?' Dillon's voice was disinterested.

Clint nodded. 'Yeah, Dyer, and he's sure told us some mighty interesting things.' Clint's eyes switched to Lear whose face was mask-like. 'Jarman's looking after him until you hear what he has to say.'

A grim smile fleeted over Lear's face at the mention of Jarman, leaving Clint with a vague sense of having missed something important.

Dillon picked up his glass and surveyed its contents with a thoughtful expression before drinking, then thrusting it back on the counter he pulled his hat forward and eased away from the bar.

'You fellers wait right here,' he growled with a sweeping glance at his crew and they relaxed against the bar readily enough.

'I guess Lear'd better tag along,' put in Mex, his mouth curving in a sneer as he stared at Dillon's segundo. 'Dyer's got plenty to say that'll be mighty interesting to him.'

Dillon jerked his head, indicating that Lear was to accompany him and the man hauled himself away from the bar with lazy grace, his basilisk eyes fixed on the Mexican's face.

Six hard-faced women came trundling out of Daniel's inner room and started up a dance routine as the four men walked out. The dancers wore long split-sided dresses that started half-way down their bosoms so nobody took much notice of the departing men. Outside, the men commenced their walk to the gaol in pairs. Mutual distrust was overcome wordlessly by Dillon walking ahead with Clint, Mex and Lear keeping pace just a couple of strides behind. No words were spoken and their footsteps sounded hollowly along the raised wooden sidewalk. A puncher staggered out of a saloon and lurched against Dillon who thrust the man aside with a curse. Clint grinned in the darkness. Dillon was beginning to have misgivings.

They were almost at the gaolhouse door when the gunshot sounded above the general night noise of Twin Springs. With his gun in his hand Clint made the door of the gaol and kicked it open. Jarman stood with smoke trickling out of his gun and Dyer lay sprawled face downwards, arms outstretched, one hand holding a gun. The other men piled in after Clint and for a moment Jarman's eyes were fastened on Lear, the last man in. Dillon looked from Jarman to Dyer than back to the marshal.

'What happened?' he barked.

Jarman replaced his gun in its holster and

calmly helped himself to a drink before replying.

'These rannies brought Dyer in at gunpoint,' he said, nodding towards Clint and Mex. 'They reckoned he had something to say that would interest you, something about rustling stock. Then they left Dyer while they fetched you.'

'And how did he get himself shot?' Mex asked. Jarman ignored the Mexican and kept his gaze on Dillon.

'Dyer was pretty worked up,' Jarman went on. 'Said these two hombres jumped him an' made him swear at gun point that he'd had a hand in rustling a herd of mixed brands; told him to swear that Lear was siding him.' Dillon's eyes were boring into the marshal and the lawman took a long drink out of his bottle.

'They swore they'd gun him down if he didn't make the story stick, an' so I told him if he was on the level he didn't have anything to worry about.' Jarman paused, keeping his eyes away from the pards with an effort. 'I guess Dyer got edgy. He didn't like his chances an' I reckon he wanted to put some distance between him an' these trouble makers. Anyway, when I got the bottle out to give him a drink an' turned away from the table, he helped himself to one of my irons an' made for the door to the cell block. He tried to open it then asked me for the key. I said no, so he made to salivate me.' Jarman shrugged. 'He was a mite slow.'

Dillon turned and surveyed the pards with cold eyes.

'Looks like things didn't work out for you hombres,' he said icily. 'I guess I can't follow what you intended to gain outa the move but you're plumb outa luck.'

'If anyone's outa luck Dillon, it's you,' retorted Clint. 'What Dyer was going to say I reckon you'll never know now until it's too late. And just for the record, no one told him what to say.'

'Huh, seems like you bustards are trying your hand at setting us to fight each other,' Lear put in, a mocking smile on his face. 'Mebbe Nugent forgot to tell you the Bar Q's a mighty tight outfit.'

There was a tinge of doubt on Dillon's face as he looked at his segundo, but Lear returned the gaze with bland unconcern.

'You hombres got anything more to say?' Dillon grunted as he switched his gaze to Clint and Mex.

'Yeah, just this Dillon,' Mex replied. 'It must be some comfort to you to have such an all-fired hell-a-miler for a segundo as this woman-beater.'

Dillon's eyes widened as Lear turned four square to stare at the Mexican.

'I sort of gathered the idea you favoured Kathy Rushland some Dillon,' Mex went on. 'It seems Lear had ideas about her too. I happened along just in time.'

The blood was mounting Dillon's face and the temper flared out of his eyes. Lear stood poised, almost trembling with eagerness to go for his guns, but the Mexican and the stock Texan were calm and unmoved.

'No gunplay! I'll drill the first man to move!' Jarman's harsh voice brought attention to the gun he had palmed so smoothly.

Lear dragged his eyes away from Mex and shrugged. 'I can wait,' he snarled. 'I'll sure enough enjoy waiting an' that's more'n can be said for you, greaser.'

Mex half turned towards Clint as if to head out of the gaol-house then he spun like greased lightning, the report from his gun coinciding with Jarman's yelp of pain as the gun was shot out of his hand. Lear's instinctive move to his gun was stayed half-way. Dillon was watchful but he made no move. Mex smiled easily and nodded towards Dyer's prone body.

'Your fingers are a mite too itchy, Jarman, for me to feel comfortable with you holding the aces. We can talk better this way.'

Jarman said nothing but his expression held only hate.

'Where's Nugent?' Mex spoke softly but the menace was there.

'He left just after you brought Dyer in,' the marshal ground out. 'He didn't say which way he was heading.' He drew his savage glance away from the mockery on the pards' faces and took refuge in pouring himself a drink.

Mex switched his attention to Dillon.

'You check on Lear with Kathy Rushland,' he suggested. 'I guess you'll take her sayso. And you Lear … don't push your luck, or you'll mebbe find the cards you're playing are all marked.'

Neither Dillon nor Lear answered but Dillon was staring hard at his segundo. Clint moved around the men removing their guns, then taking down the key from a wall hook, he unlocked the door to the cells.

'Inside,' Mex nodded towards the cell block and after a pause Dillon and Lear moved inside. 'What makes you think you're not included?' he added staring at Jarman.

The marshal was taken aback but he checked his reply and followed Dillon and Lear inside. Mex leaned idly on the door frame whilst Clint prised the gun out of Dyer's stiffening fingers and collected a Sharps from a wall bracket.

'It'll be a mite unhealthy for you hombres outside so you'd best take it easy until we clear town. We'll leave your shooting irons at the livery.'

The Mexican's tone was bantering, setting the tempers of the three men aflame. Only Dillon managed to keep himself in check.

He reckoned that with Nugent beaten, the pardners would ride right on out of the territory. He saw no sense in prolonging their stay.

'You've gone the whole hog, Mister,' Jarman snarled. 'It cuts no ice what that lawman Delahay says about you. Next time you hit town you'll rot in this hoosegow.'

'Not after I'm done with him.' Lear's voice was brittle. 'He'll rot in Boot Hill.'

Mex eased away from the door frame and kicked the door shut, then opened the front door for Clint who was carrying the gunbelts and rifles. He transferred the key from the inside to the outside of the street door and locked up.

Clint pressed on up Main Street to the livery stable whilst Mex crossed the street and stood in the shadows to keep the gaol house under observation. The minutes ticked away but no one emerged. They were taking the Mexican's warning seriously and Mex smiled as he cupped his hands to shade the light as he lit a cheroot. About ten minutes later he heard the hoofbeats above the general noise that still drifted out of the saloons and he picked out Clint's unmistakable form in the light that reached out from the Casino. Another horseman rode beside Clint but Mex was not left in doubt concerning the man's identity for long. When he stepped out of the shadows he recognized

Nugent. Clint handed the pinto's lead rein to the Mexican who swung himself into the saddle, then without a word the three men rode out of Twin Springs on the Rawlins trail.

Only when they had cleared the town did they rein in and talk. Nugent was dumbfounded when he heard of Dyer's treachery.

'I guess Dillon had the edge on me all the time,' he said as he built himself a smoke. 'When your segundo's stealing you blind I reckon your chance of keeping ahead is mighty slim.'

'The game's not played out yet,' Clint remarked. 'But it's getting mighty close to the end.'

'Huh, it's ended for me.' Nugent's tone was decisive. 'I'm sure obliged to you fellers for taking sides but there's no call to carry on the fight. I'm heading for Rawlins.'

Mex drew hard on his cheroot and searched Nugent's face in the meagre light.

'Howcome you're backing out?' he asked brusquely. 'I didn't take you for the sort of hombre who'd sneak out from under when the going got really tough.'

'I guess I owe it to you two to let you know the way of things.' Nugent spoke slowly and without rancour. 'I was aiming on settling down on the Triple Bar with Kathy Rushland for my wife.' He stubbed his cigarette out savagely. 'I seemed to think she favoured me more than Dillon but I sure enough found out my mistake. She's got it all fixed up to wed Dillon in a couple of days. I guess I can't hate her hard enough to salivate her man so I'm moving out.'

This was something the pards understood and their respect for the Triple Bar man increased in consequence. It took a mighty big man to turn his back on revenge for the sake of a woman.

'That's sure enough your business, Nugent,' Clint said at length. 'But before you head outa the territory we'd like your help.'

'You name it,' Nugent said quickly.

'I've gotta feeling that mighty soon now Lear's gonna leave town for keeps. I'd appreciate your company trailing him. Mex will stay and keep an eye on Dillon.'

'Sure thing I'll tag along. You think Lear's gonna move that herd of rustled beef outa the valley you spoke of?'

'Could be.' Clint turned his big horse round facing Twin Springs. 'Come on then,' he said. 'Let's get where we can keep tabs on anyone leaving town.'

Nugent and Mex hauled their mounts round and they headed back at an easy canter.

CHAPTER NINE

'You gonna let those hombres get away Jarman?' Dillon snarled when the street door slammed behind Mex.

Jarman glared at the Bar Q man in surprise.

'Why me?' he asked. 'I'm mebbe marshal of Twin Springs but that don't mean I risk my neck fighting your battles. If you want 'em that bad, you get 'em.'

Dillon's face went deep red as the temper rose in him.

'Your days as marshal are just about finished, Jarman,' he roared. 'You buck me and I'll get you voted out durned quick.' He turned to Lear who leaned against a cell door building himself a smoke. 'That greaser said you attacked Miss Rushland. That right?'

Lear took time to get his cigarette the right shape and alight then he looked square at his boss and Dillon was shocked by the new look on the man's face. Lear had always deferred and had given the appearance of subservience to his boss but now the man's iron will showed in every feature.

'Yeah, that's so.' He spoke softly. 'I'd have

taught the stiff-necked bitch a lesson or two if that blamed Juarez hadn't got the drop on me.' He laughed outright at the expression on Dillon's face. 'I reckon you can relax. I didn't get around to the lesson.'

Dillon didn't reply. He hurled himself at his segundo and flashed a few solid punches at the lighter man. Lear slid away from the attack, turning Dillon with some neat footwork, and countered with lightning sharp punches to the face.

Dillon steadied himself and swung a hard right into Lear's stomach then chopped two quick blows to the side of his chin as his head came down and Lear tumbled in a heap. Dillon hauled him to his feet and pumped a few more blows into the man's face then he let him drop. Jarman looked on unimpressed. He figured that Lear without a gun was a much different proposition from Lear armed. Dillon stepped away from his victim and pushing the door open to Jarman's office he went through and helped himself out of the marshal's bottle.

Lear stirred and after shaking his head a few times dragged himself to his feet. He wiped the blood away from his cut lips and split nose with his bandana, and when the strength had seeped back into his legs went through into the office. Dillon ignored him and made inroads into Jarman's bottle until the sounds of horses coming to a halt outside then setting off again told him Bellamy and Juarez had left town. He stood up, and crossing to the window kicked the frame out, sending glass fragments flying. Without a backward glance he climbed out to the sidewalk and made his way back to the Casino.

'What now?' asked Jarman as he pushed the bottle towards Lear.

Lear shrugged, his eyes on Dyer's corpse. 'I guess it's time we pulled our freight,' he said. 'We can get that herd on the move by midday tomorrow. We can collect Grant and Dewar at the Bar Q then head straight for the valley. I reckon Cawson'll be might pleased to stop kicking his heels.'

'How about Dillon? You gonna let him get away with the strong-arm stuff?' Jarman watched closely for reaction but Dillon's segundo smiled quietly with secret amusement.

'I'm not going looking for him so he'll mebbe get away with it.' Lear's smile gave way to a harsh laugh. 'But I've gotta notion he's gonna get to thinking, and he'll be burning leather to catch up with us. I'll be packing a brace of guns then.'

Jarman looked hard at Lear. He had a vague notion he was missing the drift but he knew better than to press for explanations.

Lear stood up and wiped the rest of the blood away from his face. 'You coming?' he asked, turning to look at Jarman. 'If Dillon follows then I reckon we can head back when the herd's passed on to the agent. If he doesn't then we keep on going.'

Jarman looked around the gaol-house, ignoring Dyer's body. He shrugged his shoulders. There was nothing to regret. He reckoned the dinero that would come his way when the stolen herd was passed on to the crooked Indian agent would serve him better than the wage he drew as a lawman.

'I guess so,' he replied. 'I'll be ready and waiting.'

Lear nodded and went on out through the broken window. Jarman collected up some personal effects and a thick wad of notes out of a wall safe before following Lear outside and making his way round the gaol to the stable.

'Here they come,' whispered Mex, and his two companions strained their ears to pick up the sound of hoofbeats, but a few seconds passed before they heard the oncoming riders above the whistling wind.

The moon was strong enough for Clint to pick up the light over part of the trail that stretched below the copse where the pards waited with Nugent, and when the riders emerged from between the two humped hills that stood guard over Twin Springs like sentinels they were immediately recognizable.

'That's a mighty thick saddle roll Jarman's toting,' Nugent muttered. 'Looks like he's heading out.'

'Yeah, could be,' agreed Clint as the two riders passed rapidly beyond the fringe of light. 'One thing's for sure, he ain't tracking bank robbers and killers while he's in company with Lear.'

'I guess that leaves Dillon in town,' put in Mex. 'I'll mebbe get some shut-eye after all tonight.' He moved his pinto on out of the copse down to the trail and headed for town.

Clint and Matt Nugent watched him until he passed between the hills then they too gigged their mounts out of the shadow of the trees and set after Lear and Jarman. Upon Clint's instruction Nugent had taken the precautions that were second nature to the Texan. He had fastened everything that might have made the slightest noise. His spurs were securely bound up in his saddle roll and during their wait he had oiled his saddle leather so that creaking was almost completely eliminated. They moved down on to the trail like wraiths and even when their mounts hit the hard dirt road their muffled hooves made no noise.

The moon was strong enough for Clint to pick up the trail but now and again the light was blocked by bulky rock formations and they rode with the utmost caution. Clint realised that from now on Lear would be at

171

his deadliest so he was not prepared to present himself as an easy target to the man's ever ready gun.

When they came to the point where the Bar Q trail branched off the moonlight showed up the passage of Lear and Jarman quite clearly. The two men had made no effort to obscure the sign. It appeared they were so sure of their movements that they were not one whit concerned who followed them.

Eventually Clint and Matt rode out of the long run of canyons to the open range where the trail was no more than a dusty line between the thick prairie bunch grass. They caught a glimpse of Lear and Jarman momentarily silhouetted on the top of a ridge, and Clint reached over to lay a restraining arm on Nugent.

'We've gotta move mighty carefully from here, Matt,' he whispered. 'Lear's a cagey hombre and unless we take care we'll end up looking down his gun barrels.'

'It's two to two the way I see it,' replied Nugent. 'Those are odds that suit me.'

Clint shot an exasperated glance at the Triple Bar man but he kept his temper.

'I'll trade lead with Lear and Jarman if it's gotta be that way,' he muttered. 'But I'm more concerned with keeping tabs on whatever game they're set on playing.'

Nugent nodded, accepting the fact that

Clint knew what he was doing, and when they moved off he allowed the Texan to set the pace, following behind with his eyes glued on Clint, ready to act on any sign.

They came to the ridge where Clint stopped his horse and slid to the ground. He inched forward and parted the grass to stare intently at the long wide downgrade. The moon had gained considerably in strength and Clint was able to make out the massed groups of dozing cattle. Lear and Jarman were approaching the first group. As Nugent crawled up beside him, he saw three riders emerge from the black huddle of cattle and move out to meet the two men. For a short while the five men talked in a tight group then one man separated to head in the direction of the Bar Q headquarters whilst the other four rode slowly through the groups of cattle towards the north-west.

Clint stayed where he was until it was quite evident that the four riders were keeping going. They were soon lost from sight, but from the direction they had taken he was satisfied he knew their destination. He reckoned they would keep. He was willing to bet a dime to a goldmine that Lear was the one who had made for the Bar Q headquarters, and Lear was the man he was most concerned about.

'What we've just seen proves one thing anyway,' said Clint in a voice that just carried above the wind.

'What's that?' asked Nugent.

'No matter what Jarman might have been, he's now a crooked lawman.'

As they made their way back to where their horses munched the sweet dew-moistened grass the Texan was absorbed with the proof of Jarman's defection.

'Y'know,' he said as he swung into the saddle. 'It's my bet Jarman killed Dyer deliberately to stop him saying his piece.'

Nugent was about to ask what he meant by the statement when Clint motioned him to silence again and set off downgrade. Matt Nugent grinned wryly and followed. He had a vague feeling that despite his intention to leave the field open for Dillon, things were happening that would change his mind. He regarded the Texan's broad back thoughtfully. There was solidity and dependability in every fibre of Bellamy's strong body and his pardner Juarez matched him in all aspects. They were two mighty fine men to have alongside and he knew now, suddenly, that he could not leave his range when these two would most certainly pursue their intentions to the bitter end.

Clint headed away from the groups of dozing cattle, making a wide detour. He had no wish to bump into a puncher on night trick. Gunplay now would most certainly put Lear on his guard and the Texan preferred to travel a longer distance at greater speed to minimize the risk. He knew his big dun gelding was as sure-footed in the dark as by daylight, with a built-in ability to sense gopher holes, and he hoped that Nugent's mount was as capable.

By using the terrain intelligently and indulging in occasional bursts of speed, they kept pace with their quarry. Now and again they paused and caught sight of him from cover. On one occasion they were near enough to recognize the rider. As Clint had surmised, it was Lear. Once they nearly ran into trouble. They were riding hard for a break in a ride ahead of them when the lowing of cattle disturbed from their slumber was borne downwind to them. Clint veered away from the break with Nugent in close attendance and gained the cover of a small fold. They slid out of their saddles, intending to gain the ridge on foot to take a look at what lay beyond, but instead they stayed immobile as three riders burst out of the break and headed at a smart pace to where the main herd rested.

'Phew, that was close,' Clint whispered with a grin as the riders pressed on and rapidly faded from view.

'Yeah, just half a minute later and we'd have met those hombres face to face,' Nugent replied.

'Waal, looks like our luck's in.' Clint turned

back down to his horse as he spoke. 'I guess we can ride straight through that break now.' He paused and waited for Nugent to climb into the saddle. 'By my reckoning we're getting mighty close to Dillon's ranch house now.'

'You're durned right, Clint. Another three miles nor'-west should bring us back on to the trail just before it runs down between the big grass compounds where he keeps his cavvy.'

Clint gave a satisfied nod and led the way back up out of the fold and through the break in the high ridge. A small herd stirred on the other side and a couple of restless steers gave mournful voice as the two men rode along their flanks, but there were no riders to worry about.

About twenty minutes later they joined up with the Bar Q headquarters trail just where Nugent had prophesied and Clint pointed to the sign that showed Lear to be no more than minutes ahead of them.

They rode alongside the long compound, making so little noise that even the fidgety cowponies, lying in selective groups over the length and breadth of their enclosure, made no attempt to whinny a welcome. Halfway down the track, beside the compound, a thin copse of trees stood providing a windbreak against the prevailing west wind and sheltering in some measure the ranch house and outbuildings. Clint turned his mount off the trail and into the shadow of the trees. Nugent followed without hesitation.

'As good a place as any to leave the broncs,' said Clint. 'We'll press on from here more quietly on foot. When we get down to the compound, you keep watch for Lear out front and I'll work my way to the back of the house. That way we won't miss him.'

Nugent nodded. 'That suits me. Let's go.'

Before moving off Clint checked his side-guns thoroughly, then slipping them back into their holsters he jerked his head for Nugent to follow. Everything was quiet down below and the two men made their way stealthily along the edge of the corral to the shadow of the ranch buildings. They passed between the bunkhouse and the smithy, pausing momentarily to check on the occupants of the bunkhouse. Clint was only able to count three men, most of the bunks being unoccupied.

A restless horse in the stable stamped noisily and Clint froze in the shadow of the smithy, his outstretched arm restraining Nugent from stepping out into the open. They waited until it was evident that no one had been alerted then together they crossed the moonlit square at a crouching run.

Lear's horse stood at the hitchrail below the veranda. The animal turned its head to watch the approach of the two men but it made no sound. Nugent came on to the edge of the veranda while Clint sped around the side of the house and gained the shelter of what he discovered was a paint store at the rear. There was a light showing in one of the upstairs rooms and now and again a shadow flitted across the window. Clint gained the impression that the shadow was Lear's and guessed the man was gathering his belongings together. The light went out and Clint tensed, waiting for the man's next move.

Just after Clint had seen the upstairs room go into darkness, Lear came down to the big main room. Nugent saw him clearly in the shielded light of the oil lamp he carried. The glass of the oil lamp was covered on one side by a metal shield so that its light was concentrated forward.

Matt Nugent stepped quietly on to the veranda and pressing alongside the window frame, peered through. He saw Lear move a small table alongside the wall, between the wide fireplace and the far wall then cross to a desk that stood solidly against the opposite wall. Lear opened a small drawer, took out what Nugent saw to be a key and recrossed the room. He placed the oil lamp on the table and took down a picture from the wall, exposing a small inset safe.

Lear was wholly absorbed. He turned the key and pulled the safe door open, then lifting the lamp from the table he shone its light into the safe. Judging from the satisfied smile on Lear's face, Nugent decided the contents of the safe represented a fair night's work.

Dillon's segundo proceeded to empty the safe, making a couple of journeys to the table in the middle of the room, then closing the safe he returned to the table, laying the oil lamp alongside the piled-up currency. While he bent down to pick up a pair of leather saddle-bags Nugent had a good view of the massed money.

The temper suddenly flamed into Matt Nugent. He recognized the distinctive binders around two huge wads of notes as belonging to the East National Bank and he knew for certain that the notes were his property, the money he had received in Sedalia for the sale of his trail herd. The Agency to whom he had sold the herd had completed the entire transaction through the bank. The full enormity of Dillon's duplicity struck him and the thought rushed into his mind that Dillon must be responsible for the killing of Dan Rushland and his clerk Cressy.

Matt Nugent saw red. Without counting the cost he moved to the door and thrust it open, his gun in hand.

'Stay put, Lear!' he shouted but Lear reacted with dazzling speed.

He straightened up and in one fluid movement picked up the oil lamp and sent it hurtling across the rom. Matt sent a bullet in Lear's general direction then staggered and fell as Lear drew and fired with fascile ease. The oil lamp burst into flames just a couple of feet away from Nugent's prone form and Lear thrust the money into his saddle bags hurriedly, then without a thought for Nugent rushed outside to his horse. The bunkhouse door was flung open and a couple of men emerged. Lear took immediate care of the situation.

'Get around the house, Hiram!' he shouted. 'Some hombres have been loose in the house. I've plugged one.'

'Sure thing, Don,' answered Hiram. The man's voice was thick with sleep and Lear permitted himself a grim smile as he thought how neatly he had saddled Nugent with the robbery. He had cleared the compound and was lost to sight when Clint made the front of the house. The Texan cursed Nugent's impetuosity as he guessed the Triple Bar man had rushed his fences.

The flaming oil lamp had spread its flames and the light flickered through the windows. Clint pulled himself on to the veranda and made to rush to the door but Hiram spotted him from the bunkhouse and sent a couple of bullets crashing into the woodwork so close to the Texan that he felt the wind of their passage. Clint threw himself down on the veranda and slammed three shots in

180

rapid succession at the point of Hiram's gun-flash and a foot to either side. As he rolled away nearer to the door, he heard the man's grunt as one of the bullets found its mark. Then a couple more guns took up the battle.

A bullet ploughed up the floorboards just an inch from Clint's face and another tugged its way through the rim of his hat making him decide to get amongst Dillon's men in an attempt to bring the gunplay to an end. Dropping down from the veranda he made for the bunkhouse in a swerving run. At the same time that the moonlight revealed him he saw the two shadowy forms on either side of the bunkhouse. He pitched full length into the dust as a rapid tattoo of gunshots sprayed bullets at stomach height. There was a split second delay while he fired with both guns and as the dust cleared he saw both men reel out of their meagre cover and fall to the ground.

Clint stayed where he was for a full minute until he was sure that no further danger lurked near, then conscious of the fire that had taken hold of the ranch house he hauled himself upright and rushed to the house to look for Nugent. Kicking the door open he coughed as the smoke swirled out. The rush of air fanned the flames that had already taken hold and the dry timber work crackled as it fed the spreading fire.

Nugent lay where he had fallen. Flames

licked the floorboards just a few inches away from his face and Clint saw the dark stain spreading beside him. He eased the Triple Bar man away from the flames then turned him over gently to explore the wound. Nugent was still alive and Clint grunted with relief. A quick look at the jagged wound in the youngster's side told him that skilled aid would be needed pretty soon.

With great care Clint picked Nugent up and carried him outside and across the compound where he laid him down. Then, the need for speed uppermost in his mind the Texan ran back to the copse where the horses waited. Taking the lead rein of Nugent's horse, Clint jumped into the saddle and rode down to the compound.

The fire had taken hold now and the high wind was fanning the flames, spreading light over a wide area. Clint slid to the ground and unfastened his warbag to get the bandage rolls he invariably carried. Cutting away the clothing from around Nugent's wound he made a thick pad and hurriedly bandaged it in place. While he worked Nugent regained consciousness, his first tentative move bringing a grunt of pain to his lips.

'Could be worse,' said Clint encouragingly as he saw the Triple Bar man's eyelids flutter.

'Did you get him?' Pain made Nugent's voice hoarse and Clint motioned him to silence.

'Nope, he got clean away. The gunplay brought the rest of the hands horning in so I just had to stay an' calm 'em down some.'

There was respect in Nugent's pain-wracked eyes as he looked up at Clint. This square-shouldered young Texan was sure some humdinger. Then he switched his attention to the flaming ranch house. His mouth twisted in a wry grin. Dillon was sure getting it hot and strong tonight. First the robbery by Lear and now his house going up in flames.

'Think you'll be able to ride back to town?' asked Clint, making the bandage fast.

Nugent nodded. 'I guess so.' He paused, then: 'Sorry I horned in on Lear when I did. I reckon I should've waited for him to leave.'

Clint shrugged and stood up to look at the ranch house and outbuildings. The stables were pretty close to the ranch house and he reckoned the heat would be enough to set it on fire before very much longer if the sparks did not do so earlier. He could hear the stamping of nervous horses above the roar of the flames and with a sign to Nugent he hurried to the stable door. Throwing it open wide he went inside. Nine boxes were occupied by Dillon's best horses and Clint talked, patted and soothed the trembling animals as he unhitched their head stalls.

One after another they backed out of their boxes and, encouraged by Clint, headed through the door to safety and freedom. As the last one departed the thatched roof burst alight and Clint ran back out to the compound. He concluded that the paint store at the rear would be enveloped in flames but the bunkhouse and smithy would escape unless the wind veered and sent sparks flying across the compound. He reckoned too that unless the wind carried sparks at high level to the copse of trees a couple of hundred yards to the west there was little danger of a prairie fire and with some relief he crossed to the bunkhouse to check on the men who had done battle with him.

Two were dead, but one a wispy, middle-aged man, was just drawing himself up on his knees, a dazed expression on his face and with blood dripping from a gash in the side of his head. Clint drew a gun and placed the muzzle against the man's forehead. He watched the man's eyes mirror returning memory, pain then fear.

'One lie and you're buzzard meat,' Clint said in a cold matter of fact voice. He stepped back. 'Get up!'

The man dragged himself to his feet, staggered and pitched forward again, then took a long time to haul himself back upright. He leaned against the bunkhouse wall and looked piteously at his tormentor.

'What's your moniker?' Clint barked the question.

'Jem Sanders.' The reply came slowly.

'You ever see a prospector and a burro on the Bar Q?' Clint raised his gun again and his face was devoid of expression.

'Yeah-heah,' Sanders muttered, exploring his scalp with his fingers. 'Old Dinny Lever rode in a coupla months back from the Teton Mountains on a flea-bitten pony. His burro was tagging along.'

'Where's Lever now?'

'He was sick when he hit the spread,' Sanders replied, his eyes rivetted on his hand, red with his own blood. 'He died after a coupla days. He's buried up there just below the trees.'

'And his bronc and burro?'

'Funny thing about 'em,' said Sanders. 'Dave Cawson took 'em away some time later. He'd let his face fungus grow that long, danged if he didn't look like a sourdough himself.'

'You're doing all right, Sanders,' Clint said quietly. 'A couple more questions. Did you ride into town the day Rushland and Cressy were murdered?'

'I ain't been in town in two months, Mister,' Sanders replied. 'I get lumbered with the chores.'

'This Cawson, has he been back since he left with Lever's outfit?'

'Sure, turned up a couple days ago, all spruced up without the face fungus. Then he

185

headed out again with his warbag.' Sanders took time out to survey the blazing ranch house and stables. It was getting mighty hot and the perspiration pumped out of both men.

'You think back to the day of the bank raid,' insisted Clint. 'How many hands were left on the Bar Q?'

Sanders winced as his brow furrowed in thought. 'The way I heard it, the bank was likely raided a day before Rushland and Cressy was found,' he said. 'The day they was found most everybody was right here but for a coupla days before, most of the regular guntoters was somewhere else.'

Clint holstered his gun and the fear went out of Sanders' eyes.

'If you want to come into town, you're welcome,' the Texan said. 'You can get that wound patched up, and if you want, I reckon Matt Nugent will fix you up with top hand pay. Otherwise I'd advise you to ride into the sun. Anybody forking a bronc for Dillon is likely to be dead pretty soon.'

Sanders looked again at the blazing house. He grinned for the first time. 'I'll ride into town,' he said. 'There's sure nothing to stay on for.'

CHAPTER TEN

When Mex arrived back in town he made straight for the livery stable and after bedding his pinto down returned to Main Street, keeping at all times in the shadows. He was in luck for as soon as he arrived alongside the Casino's batwing doors and peered in, Lew Dillon pushed his way through the bunch of punchers surrounding him at the bar and walked through the intervening door to the hotel section. Mex slipped quietly from the sidewalk and watched the Casino from the other side of the street for a half-hour or so. During this time a succession of punchers passed in and out but there was no sign of Dillon, and Mex concluded he had hit the hay. Nothing loth, he made his way to Seth Harben's hotel and followed Dillon's head.

At sun-up, Mex had breakfast and was leaning against the doorframe of Harben's hotel, eyeing the town carefully. The stage pulled out for Rawlins, a heavy schooner drew round in front of the hardware store drawn by two deep chested horses and the driver banged at the door until it was flung open. A couple of punchers staggered out of the Casino and unfastening their mounts from the hitchrail hauled themselves into their saddles, heading out of town towards Rawlins. They rode their mounts like sacks of hay and Mex reckoned they would ride half-way to Rawlins before the effects of the night's drinks wore off. A few men crossed the street and pushed their way into the Chinese Chop House. The scene was just what one would expect in any Western cattle town and Mex treated himself to a cheroot to ease the boredom.

Seth Harben came alongside him and tried to make conversation but Mex was non-committal and the hotel keeper grunted and finally left him alone. Mex grinned at the man's back and returned his gaze to the town.

Dillon took his time to emerge. It was a couple of hours after sun-up when the Bar Q man stepped out on to the sidewalk from the Casino's hotel entrance. He extracted a cigar from the inside pocket of his Prince Albert and lit up with deliberate care. Mex eased back inside the doorway a little so that he was hidden but still had Dillon under observation.

A couple of minutes later he saw Kathy Rushland walking along the raised sidewalk on the other side of the street. She caught sight of Dillon and Mex saw her expression change to one of strain and distaste. She looked away and hurried into the store. A few minutes went by and Dillon crossed the road to the store. When Kathy Rushland returned to the sidewalk Dillon was right beside her, his arm round her slim shoulders. Kathy was looking straight ahead but Mex could see she had difficulty in keeping up any appearance of friendliness with the Bar Q man.

Mex chewed his cheroot thoughtfully. For his money Nugent was wrong one thing. Kathy certainly did not favour Dillon any.

'Tell Lear to get the boys in the saddle an' heading for the Bar Q.' Dillon's harsh voice thundered out to a puncher who had just walked stiff-legged out of the Casino. Mex grinned as he waited for the reaction and he chanced a glance around the door frame to watch the puncher shrug his shoulders then spread his hands eloquently.

'Lear ain't been back in the Casino all night,' he replied.

Dillon stared across at the puncher for a full minute then with a muttered word to the girl at his side he jumped down from the sidewalk to the road.

'Get every man into the saddle, Mungo,' he shouted. 'We'll be riding mighty soon.'

The puncher turned abruptly and pushed his way through the batwing doors back into the Casino while Dillon headed for the gaol house. Kathy Rushland crossed the street quickly and Mex saw her fumble with the key then disappear into the bank.

When Dillon entered the gaol Mex slipped out of the doorway of Harben's hotel and sped along the sidewalk to the bank. He was in luck. No one saw him and he pushed the door open just enough to slip inside, then bolted the door behind him.

Kathy Rushland had just sat down at her desk when Mex rushed in. She pushed the chair back and stood up, staring at him but the Mexican smiled and placing a warning finger to his lips, he went to the window. The girl looked at his back uncertainly for a moment then joined him. They drew back as Dillon went rushing past, his face like thunder. Mex laughed and moved away from the window to the middle of the office. Kathy followed him.

'What's going on?' she asked, pushing her blonde curls away from her forehead.

Mex sat on the edge of her desk and gave her a hard look.

'You tell me something first,' he said. The girl's lovely big blue eyes fastened on his face and she nodded for him to continue. 'Would you marry Lew Dillon if Matt Nugent could stay on this range without risking his life?'

Kathy Rushland gasped and the colour mounted her face as the Mexican's shrewd question took her off guard. She regarded him frankly and shook her head.

'That's the way I figured,' Mex said kindly. 'Now Matt reckons you prefer Dillon anyway and he's vacating this range rather than risk killing your man.'

Kathy's eyes dropped and her hand went to her throat in a nervous gesture.

'He's got to think that way to leave the territory,' she said. 'That way and I'll know he's safe.'

Mex stood up and walked around a bit then he came back and faced her.

'Right now Matt Nugent and Clint Bellamy are trailing Lear and Jarman who are heading for a trail herd they've rustled and cached in a valley hidden in the hills.' Mex jerked his head towards the street where the dust spilled up as Dillon's men swept out of town. 'Dillon's got his own reasons for going after Lear and that's what he's getting out to do right now. That puts Nugent and Bellamy in between Lear and Dillon. Nugent was all set for leaving the territory and he's only riding along with Bellamy because he reckons he owes us a favour.'

The colour drained from Kathy Rushland's face as she visualized Nugent being caught between two fires, then she steadied herself as the Mexican's calm manner impressed itself upon her.

'I guess you'd do best, Ma'am by letting Nugent know the truth the first time you can and let him take his chance against

Dillon's outfit.'

As Mex spoke he walked to the window. Dillon went past at that moment riding hard in the wake of his men. Mex moved to the door.

'Where are you going now?' Kathy's voice was firm.

'On Dillon's trail Ma'am.' The Mexican's tone was bland.

'I'm coming with you,' the girl replied. Mex shrugged resignedly. His instincts told him she would come to no harm.

'Let's go,' he said. 'It'll be a pleasure to have some good company along for once. You're some improvement on Bellamy.'

'You're only being polite,' she answered. 'I've gathered the impression you and Bellamy are mighty good pardners.'

Mex smiled and nodded as he held the door open for her.

The sun came up very shortly after Clint rode with the two wounded men away from the gutted Bar Q. Nugent hung on desperately to his saddle pommel, his face drained of colour and wracked in pain. Sanders, too, looked as though his scalp wound was giving him trouble. Clint had bandaged the Bar Q man's head but the man's eyes were dulled as though he was suffering from delayed concussion.

All the time Clint kept a watchful eye on

Nugent. Now and again he rode alongside, imparting moral support, getting a wry smile in return but for the most part he rode just behind where he could observe the youngster more carefully. He did not think that any vital organ had been damaged by the bullet but he had no doubt that Nugent had many painful weeks in front of him before he would again ride in comfort.

The pace was restricted to the maximum of Nugent's capacity which was no more than a jogtrot and although Clint allowed no trace of his concern to show, he cursed inwardly at having to wet-nurse the two men back to town when he wanted to be on Lear's trail. Nugent had been silent all the way, conserving every vestige of energy for the long ordeal ahead, but just before they entered the long canyon that led out of Dillon's range to the Twin Springs trail, he caught Clint's eye as the Texan came alongside.

'Y'know Clint,' he gasped. 'I horned in on Lear when I saw him robbing Dillon's safe.' Clint cast a sharp eye on him and waited. 'Part of the money he took outa that safe was the dinero I'd handed to Rushland for safe-keeping.' Nugent forestalled Clint's question. 'My money was stached in two piles and fastened with East National Bank binders,' he added.

'I reckoned there was a mighty good

reason for trying your hand against Lear,' Clint replied. 'But don't let things worry you. We'll catch up with Lear in good time.'

Nugent seemed satisfied and he relapsed into silence, hunched uncomfortably in the saddle, trying to ease the pounding pain that throbbed through his side at each step his mount took. Clint dropped back again and gave himself over to a new evaluation of the situation in the light of what both Nugent and Sanders had told him. He found cause for satisfaction in the fact that events were proving he and Mex had been on the right track from the start.

They finally broke out of the lengthy canyon on to the town trail, then as they reached the head of a steep draw Clint, who was riding alongside Nugent, saw the dust cloud rising a mile or so below them as many riders headed for the Bar Q. He leaned over, taking hold of Nugent's lead rein, and hauled the Triple Bar man's horse around at the same time barking an order at the still dazed Jem Sanders. There was cover enough alongside the trail and Clint led them into a ring of junipers.

The hoofbeats became audible and soon about twenty riders flashed past them on the trail just below. Dillon was there, right in front, riding in dedicated fashion, eyes straight ahead, grim purpose in every line of his body. The dust spilled up, obliterating the riders as they moved quickly towards the canyon that led to the Bar Q. Clint smiled with savage enjoyment as he pictured Dillon's reaction upon reaching the burned-out ranch house. As the hoofbeats died away he led the pair back on to the trail and down the long draw.

Nugent was sinking lower in the saddle as the hot sun added discomfort to his pain and Clint began to doubt whether in fact the Triple Bar man would be able to make town after all. He was just considering sending Sanders on in for a wagon and the doctor when they rounded a bend and the signal he and Mex used shrilled from above the trail. Clint held on to Nugent's horse, pulling it to a stop, and turned to welcome his pard. He started with surprise as Kathy Rushland rode down the steep hillside just behind Mex's pinto.

Clint and Mex greeted each other briefly with upraised hands then both turned in the saddle to watch Kathy Rushland ride alongside Nugent and lean over to him, searching his face for an indication of the gravity of his wound.

'Oh, Matt – Matt!' she cried. 'Is it bad?'
His eyes that had been slitted with pain opened a little more and he tried a smile but it fell short into little better than a grimace.

'Not that bad I can't ride into town,' he gasped.

Kathy shot a panic-stricken glance at Clint who nodded.

'Yeah, I guess he'll make it all right if you ride nice and easy,' he said. 'Get him into a bed at Harben's and get the doctor to dig out the slug pronto.' His latter remark was calculated and he turned way to grin at the girl's hot reply.

'Matt Nugent's not going to lie wounded in Seth Harben's filthy hotel,' she flared. 'I'm taking him to my place where I can see he'll be looked after properly.'

A brief smile of pleasure flitted over Matt Nugent's face as the girl's remark filtered through his bemused mind and he took a firmer grip on his saddle pommel.

'You'd better get going then,' Clint put in. 'I guess it's up to you to get Nugent into Twin Springs. Mex and me have got work to do.' He looked thoughtfully at Jem Sanders who seemed to be recovering with every passing minute. 'If you want to earn that job on the Triple Bar, Sanders,' he said. 'You'd better hightail it into town and get the doc stirred up ready and it'll sure help some if you get a wagon moving out in case Nugent finds he can't ride any further.'

'Righto Mister, I'll do just that,' Sanders replied and without further ado set his mount off downtrail.

Kathy Rushland sent a grateful look to Clint and Mex who had sat quietly smoking throughout, an amused glint in his eye. She reached over to take Nugent's lead rein.

'Matt'll have some interesting things to tell you, Ma'am, when he gets around to talking, and tell him we're aiming on bringing things to a head mighty soon now,' said Clint.

'Thank you both,' Kathy said, her eyes suddenly moist. 'And do be careful.'

She urged her mount forward taking Nugent's horse along. Nugent was hunched up in the saddle trying to press away the pain that pounded through his side. He was beyond notice of his surroundings and only hung on to his saddle by instinct.

'Reckon he'll make it,' he replied. 'But he'll be about all in when he hits town. I don't think the bullet hit anything that matters much but he's gonna have pain enough until it's dug out. I reckon he'd stand a better chance of escaping permanent injury if a medico did the job.'

Mex nodded and tossed his matches over to Clint who was searching desultorily for his own.

'One problem's settled anyway,' he said with a grin. 'And that's who gets the girl.' He caught the matches when Clint returned them and gigged his pinto forward. 'Well, let's get going. I'm mighty interested in finding out what's on the end of this trail.'

Clint's gelding followed in the wake of the

pinto and when they drew abreast, the Texan brought Mex up to date with all that had happened.

'It's like we figured,' Mex said slowly when Clint had recounted the whole story. 'But it still don't tell us why Dillon wants the Triple Bar so badly.'

Clint shrugged. 'Mebbe we'll never know. I reckon it'll be enough to settle Dillon's hash for the killing of Rushland and his clerk.'

'Huh, that's a mighty tough assignment,' Mex grunted. 'He's sided by a score of hard-looking gunslingers.'

This fact did not appear to depress either man unduly and they rode along the well-defined trail as cheerfully as though a barbecue awaited them at the end of the journey. They entered the long canyon, enjoying the temporary relief from the rays of the hot sun but when the canyon changed course and narrowed, the reflected heat from the rock face on either side was greater than upon the open range where the incessant wind helped to minimize the sun's intensity.

Once out of the canyon they struck south-west. Neither man spoke his intention to change course but such was their mutual understanding and so acutely tuned was their sense of direction that it was by no accident they headed the same way together.

A line of small hills lay ahead of them, then beyond the undulating prairie, intersected by the river that worked its way back on to Triple Bar range almost to the foot of the bigger distant hills from whence it sprung. A dead straight line would take the pards to the entrance they had found to the hidden valley. They intended to make the valley way ahead of Dillon and his men who had, according to the sign headed for the Bar Q headquarters.

At the river they stopped, allowing their mounts to drink and to munch the lush bunch grass, while they opened a couple of cans of pork and beans and shared the pack Kathy Rushland had hurriedly prepared before she and Mex left town. They had time enough. No matter how Dillon and his crew burned leather after Lear, the pards were at least an hour and a half ahead.

They used up half an hour of their lead relaxing in readiness for whatever might arise. After eating they lay beside the river, smoking and dozing. When they eventually climbed back into their saddles, they were completely refreshed.

CHAPTER ELEVEN

'They've been mighty careless,' Mex grunted, pointing to the trail so blatantly left by the riders who had recently passed that way.

Clint nodded his agreement. 'Yeah, it looks to me as though Lear's inviting Dillon to follow him. He must be pretty sure of his chances.'

The pards pulled their mounts to a halt and glanced at each other meaningly. If Lear was laying in wait for Dillon then they would have to move with extreme caution.

The entrance to the cut lay just beyond them and as they unfastened their saddle rolls for the padded leather hoof muffles they memorized the lay of the cut to where the hidden valley opened out.

'Only about three places where anyone'd get a clear view down into the cut from above,' mused Clint as both men busied themselves fastening the muffles on to the hooves of their disgruntled horses.

'That's what I figured,' replied Mex. 'A war party riding hell-for-leather would fall straight into the trap, but I guess we can cover each other along those stretches.'

Before climbing back into the saddle both men checked their side-arms and rifles, then when satisfied they were on their way. The daylight almost vanished as they rounded the first bend in the cut and they took up their positions automatically; Clint in the lead and Mex some way behind, his trusty Sharps at the ready. The Texan had complete and utter faith in Mex Juarez. If anything stirred on either side of the trail he knew the Mexican would notice and react with the speed of a rattler. At each bend they paused together while Mex observed the run beyond and only when he was satisfied that he was positioned to provide complete safety to Clint did he motion the Texan forward.

Painstakingly they traversed almost the entire length of the cut until just one more bend lay between them and the blank cliff face that looked so much like a dead end. Once more they drew rein and surveyed both walls of the cut. Nothing moved and Mex nodded Clint forward. The Texan edged his big mount around the bend and made for the huge boulders that lay humped like fallen cathedral domes at the foot of the blank face.

Something moved at the highest point of the left-hand wall and Mex brought his Sharps to bear like lightning. It was the merest suggestion of movement and for the moment no real target presented itself.

Clint's gelding kept padding its steady muffled way up the middle of the cut.

A breathless minute passed and the Texan was almost abreast of the hidden exit from the cut when Mex saw the rifle barrel snake down between two humps of rock at the top and move horizontally to line up on Clint. For a split second a face showed behind the rifle, lining up the sights, and in that instant Mex fired. Clint slid down one side of his mount and rode Indian fashion for the shelter of the boulders while from above him came a sharp scream and then the rifle clattered into view and bounced a few times before hitting the ground with a crash.

Mex and Clint stayed immobile for some time while the reverberating echoes died away and a pall of silence settled down upon them. Tentatively Clint emerged, sixguns in hand, but nothing moved above them. He stepped out into the open, inviting enemy fire, but poised on elastic taut muscles to seek cover at the first sign of trouble. His pent-up breath whistled away as the tension eased and Mex rode down to meet him.

'Nice shooting Mex,' Clint muttered. 'I guess that hombre up there could have meant curtains for one of us anyways.'

'He sure obliged me some by showing himself,' returned Mex. 'Let's go take a look-see.'

The Mexican dismounted and led his

pinto behind a boulder alongside Clint's gelding, then together the pards climbed the difficult rock wall.

It was a tough climb and they were sweating streams by the time they gained the top. The Mexican's aim had been dead on target and the corpse stretched full length was not a pretty sight. Recognition would have been difficult even for a close relative and the pard's curiosity did not stretch as far as identity. The dead man's function was all that interested them.

A small shaving mirror lay beside the dead man and they guessed that down in the hidden valley, picketed out of sight, a horse waited for a rider who would never arrive. The significance of the shaving mirror struck both men simultaneously and they took new interest in their surroundings.

They stood at a high point and around them the mountains ranged in huddled profusion. Away to the south-west a deep break showed in a hump-backed mountain. Anyone watching from the break could easily pick up a signal flashed by mirror from this point.

'Y'know Clint,' said Mex, pointing to the distant break. 'That hidden valley below could quite easily continue clear through this hill and carry on between those table-topped twins then to the other side of the one with the split.'

The Texan's eyes followed the route indicated and he nodded slowly. 'Yeah, you could be right at that Mex.' He paused and considered for a while. 'If that's so,' he continued. 'Then Lear's intending to draw Dillon all the way to where that break cuts into the valley. That makes it safe for us to go on quite a piece.'

'That's hoss sense,' agreed Mex. 'Anyway this hombre sent his message. Enough of him moved to bring him to my notice a minute or so before he got you in his sights. I reckon he thought you were scouting ahead for Dillon's war party and flashed his message, then when that cayuse of yours moved so quietly he changed his mind and took you to be on your lonesome. He opined he'd play safe by sending you to Boot Hill.'

Having sorted the situation out to their satisfaction the pards buried the dead man under a pile of loose stones and climbing back down the rock wall to the cut below, collected their horses and rode along the concealed exit and on up to the point that spiralled down to the hidden valley. Some time later they rode through lush knee-high grass in the valley where rustled cattle had grazed and grown fat.

Over the centuries the rich alluvial soil had been washed down into the valley by countless rivulets from the craggy heights on each side and had formed a deep bed where the grass had taken root and flourished, and now, when the rain clouds broke over the mountains, the grass absorbed the cascading water.

'Sure is good graze.' Mex swept his gaze around the towering heights and back to the valley. 'But a mighty bad place to run a spread.'

'A man might live out a lifetime here and see no grief,' he continued. 'But sure as Hades every now and again, mebbe centuries apart, this valley gets plumb full of water and every living thing in it gets carried away.'

Clint gave a mock apprehensive glance at the sky. 'You're durned right so often, I sure hope we miss out on the proof.'

Sure enough the valley turned and twisted its way through the hill, falling always in a steady gradient until it left the vast glooming walls and widened as it passed between the table-topped mountains Mex had indicated earlier. Now it veered in a half circle and straightened out to sou'sou'west.

Riders and cattle had passed this way not so long before them and the pards rode in watchful fashion. They hugged the foot of the hillside, keeping to whatever shadow they could find. Although neither man expected trouble yet, their instinct told them that any ambush being prepared for Dillon would be at a point where the valley was much narrower.

For an hour they rode between the table-topped mountains then the humped-back mountain with the break running through its middle came into view. The pards reined in their mounts and stared hard at the terrain stretching before them. The valley disappeared between the hump back and a gaunt craggy hill, narrowing to no more than trail width. Clint wiped the perspiration out of his eyes and glanced significantly at his companion.

'I guess that's it,' he said and turned his attention to the humped-back hill on their left. It was scaleable enough to just beyond the timber. 'We should get a mighty fine view from up there.'

Mex said nothing but his sharp eyes were busy on the mountain side, sorting out the route that would keep them covered at all times from watchers lying in wait for Dillon's crew. Clint left him to it. He was content to follow the Mexican when stealth and range craft were necessary. He rarely put a foot wrong himself but Mex Juarez had no peers.

The Mexican jerked his head, indicating he was ready, and Clint grinned back at him, showing his readiness, then with Mex in the lead they picked their cautious way up the difficult slopes. Clint's admiration for Mex increased as he continued up the mountainside. Not once until they finally drew rein on the fringe of the timber did he obtain a view of the valley where it funnelled to its narrowest, so anyone watching from that vantage point would have seen nothing of their movements.

They dismounted and led their horses deeper into the tree belt, then leaving them ground hitched, returned to the cover of the trees on the edge and took up position against a fallen tree stump. The heat haze shimmered over the grassland below and now and again distorted the vision, but for the most part the pards enjoyed a good view. They relaxed, content to wait for Dillon to show up and set the ball rolling.

Time passed slowly but neither man fretted. It was sheer luxury resting in the shade, watching the long grass in the valley ripple before the wind like the waves on an inland sea. They were sufficiently removed from the point where Dillon would pass that smoking was permissible and Clint forebore to grumble at Juarez' cheroot for once as he built himself successive cigarettes.

A couple of hours went by and their vantage point lost its savour as the sun passed its zenith and shone down upon them in all its brassy strength. To keep the valley in full view they were unable to move deeper into the timber so they pulled their sombreros forward to cover their faces as much as possible and sweated things out.

'If that hombre flashed his message Lear's gonna think he made a mistake by now,' Mex said at length. 'Dillon should've been running into that bottleneck an hour ago.'

Clint was about to reply when the Mexican's restraining arm kept him quiet. The Texan strained his ears to pick up the sounds that held Mex's attention, but almost half a minute ticked away before the muted drumming of hoofbeats reached his level of hearing. They exchanged satisfied glances.

'I sure hope Lear's waiting for 'em,' Clint remarked, his eyes riveted upon the foot of the distant mountain at the point where Dillon's riders, following the course of the valley, would break into view.

Mex considered a long time before replying, but when he did his voice held conviction.

'Lear'll be waiting,' he said. 'The only reason that they don't fight it out is because they're still in cahoots, but if that's so Dillon would do no more than break even because his share of the rustled stock and the dinero Lear took from his safe would stack up no more than the value of the stock still eating the grass on the Bar Q. Nope, it's like we always figured, give the bad hombres enough time and coaxing and they'll always help out by fighting each other.'

Clint nodded; the Mexican's opinion confirmed his own entirely.

The heat haze shimmered up in the distance, shortening the horizon, then cleared again just as a huddle of black dots seemed to separate from the foot of the neighbouring hill and move out into the valley.

'Here they come,' Clint muttered. 'They're riding those cayuses mighty hard.'

'Yeah, Dillon's that hot tempered he hasn't taken time out to think. He's all worked up to reach Lear before nightfall, instead of taking things easy and making sure he'd wait for nightfall.' He grinned and his white teeth gleamed in the sunlight. 'Temper is sure something to keep in your pocket.'

The dots grew bigger until they were recognizable as horses and riders, and at last the pards were able to pick out Dillon's tall figure astride his big bay gelding. Steam rose up from the twenty or so horses in a cloud that lost itself in the heat haze, and the hunched riders were pushing their mounts to keep up the killing pace that Dillon was holding. The Bar Q men swept past, heading unerringly for the bottleneck ahead of them.

Clint and Mex kept the riders in sight as they dwindled in size to become no more than moving dots again, the tension building up in them with every passing second. Normally calm under pressure, they found that the impending action between unrelated factions gave rise to an excitement never experienced when they were themselves involved.

The dots moved into the bottleneck and were lost to sight, and the pards stared hard into the impenetrable depths unwilling to lose sight of Dillon and his men. Many minutes passed and lesser men would have doubted the strength of their reasoning but suddenly the faint sounds of distant gunfire vindicated them. There was no cessation in the rate of fire and the pards exchanged glances.

'They're mighty promiscuous with their lead,' mused Clint. 'Sounds like a running fight yet I'd have thought Lear would have taken them from cover.'

The firing continued but it seemed to be moving towards them, and the answer dawned upon both men together.

'My God! Lear's stampeding the herd back through that bottleneck!' Clint exclaimed.

The two men stood up and stared hard into the haze, straining to bring the action within their range, but for a few minutes they saw nothing. Then suddenly the black mass spilled out of the bottleneck and the drumming of hooves sounded above the gunfire.

It was impossible to separate horsemen from steers as the black mass swarmed into the widening valley, and the herd had travelled half the distance from the bottleneck to the point directly below the pards before they saw daylight between a crouching horseman and the stampede leaders. The rider kept his lead, edging all the time away from the middle of the valley towards the hillside. A few more horse-riders broke away from the far flank of the herd and tried to claw clear. The pards saw two horses stumble and go under the mad bone-crushing mass, the others drew away and turned their horses in a wide circle to get behind the herd.

The ground shuddered as the crazed herd thundered past, dust rising above them in an enveloping cloud. A long way behind them were the riders who had triggered off the stampede, in no apparent hurry to regain control. The lone rider who had made the safety of the hillside just a few hundred yards away came on up the hill to the timber. As the pards had guessed, it was Dillon.

As the dust drifted back down the valley, so the pounding hooves hurried the compact huddle of beeves ever onward in the senseless urgent rush that only sheer exhaustion would stop. Along the centre of the valley in the wake of the vanishing herd, lay the pulverized unrecognizable mounds of flesh and bone, steers that had stumbled, and perhaps horses and men who had ridden in desperation along with the herd when caught up in the stampede.

Dillon was out of sight in the shelter of the

tree belt but his remaining men, the four who had successfully broken away from the herd, were closing in on Lear's faction and the guns were blazing again. The odds were well in Lear's favour. The stampede had done its deadly work and decimated the force Dillon had taken into the bottleneck.

A running fight ensued, bringing the contestants ever nearer the vantage point where Clint and Mex watched with undisguised interest. They saw five men fall from their saddles, bringing the odds to seven to two, then out of the timber the staccato bark of a rifle brought its warning of death and a man tumbled to the ground.

Dillon was in deadly earnest. Time and again his rifle barked and horses ran on riderless. The pards saw Lear skilfully place Dillon's men between him and the marksman on the hillside while the rest of his men bit the dust. On he rode until well out of rifle range, then abruptly he turned to meet his two pursuers. Before they had a chance to ride wide of him his guns claimed them.

The pardners gazed down upon the scene of carnage almost disbelieving the evidence so gruesomely arraigned before them. They were so stunned by the magnitude of the slaughter in so short a space of time that when Dillon burst out of the timber and headed downhill for the valley, they took some time to realize that this was their clue to move and keep abreast of events.

Lear sat his horse like a statue for a brief spell, his face turned to where Dillon's gelding hit the plain then he hauled his mount round and rode away fast in the wake of the departed herd. Dillon's heels were drumming into his mount's side when he finally passed out of sight.

Soberly Clint and Mex collected their horses and climbed into their saddles. The memory of the battle they had witnessed would remain with them a long time, and when they rode slowly down into the valley their minds were too full to permit speech. The sun glinted on something some distance away. Clint saw the flash and drew the Mexican's attention to the reflected sunlight quickly.

'That's no gunbarrel,' Mex remarked. 'So I guess we can take a looksee.'

They turned and rode towards the glinting metal, albeit carefully, but there was no danger, and there was no pity on the faces of Clint and Mex when they stared down at the star glittering on the breast of the dead marshal of Twin Springs. Clint slid out of the saddle, and unfastening the badge transferred it to his pocket.

'He ain't got no right to tote that badge. Being dead don't make him a good marshal. Huh, crooked lawmen are poison.'

CHAPTER TWELVE

The trail was easy enough to follow. Lear had ridden wide of the path the stampeding cattle had taken in order to avoid the odd steer that had faltered and died under the pulverizing hooves of its fellows. Dillon kept close to Lear's trail and between them they had left enough evidence of their passing to make following him child's play. The pards were in no hurry. It was enough that they kept doggedly behind the two men.

'If that blamed herd keeps on going much longer, they'll end up on Triple Bar graze,' said Mex after the two men had ridden in silence for about an hour. 'If they get as far as the beginning of the valley, I reckon we can coax 'em the rest of the way.'

'They'll surely be a skinny-looking lot of mavericks by the time they run 'emselves out,' Clint grunted. 'It'll take a year of good grazing to get the meat back on 'em.'

Mex nodded and eased his pinto's speed. Clint checked his own mount, at the same time flashing a questioning look at his companion.

'Dillon's just ahead,' the Mexican warned. 'I caught a sight of him rounding that bend.

He's a mighty good hand with that rifle o' his so we'd better give him plenty of space.'

'Yeah, he sure made every bullet count back there. It looks like Lear's got an almighty respect for Dillon. He wasn't too keen to take a chance on getting close enough to use his six-guns.'

They were downwind of their quarry so they waited and smoked until it seemed safe to go on. They reasoned that Dillon would not linger overlong to ambush them even if he had seen them, because his prime purpose was to catch up with Lear and recover what his segundo had stolen from his safe.

The table-topped mountains were now behind them and the valley curved ever upwards at a steady but hardly noticeable incline into the mountain where it originated and where countless years ago the glacier had started its slow gouging slide that split the mountain from near its peak to the plains.

There were no more mangled carcasses and that fact told the pards the stampede as such had finished. The animals had run themselves out and now, some way ahead, they would be travelling at no more than a half-hearted lumbering run. When they came alongside the place where the dozen or so tiny streams cascaded down the side of the rock face, they would stop and with good graze at hand they would stay.

It now became difficult work trailing two riders in the wake of the herd and at times Mex was hard put to be positive that Lear and Dillon were still ahead of them. Not that the steep sides gave them much option regarding direction, but the pards never took anything for granted and all the time their sharp eyes searched for sign.

It was this painstaking attention to detail that paid off. Dillon's mount must have been far gone and now and again they found foam specks adhering to the bruised flattened grass. Then Mex spotted two rapidly diminishing flecks almost at right angles to the trail. This was enough to make the pards haul off to take a closer look.

In a direct line they saw an opening in the left-hand wall that brooded over the valley, and cautiously they rode over to check upon its possibilities as another exit. They exchanged significant glances when they saw that the opening widened just beyond the entrance and that shod horses had passed that way just a short while before.

There was nothing for it but to fix the muffles on their mounts' hooves so they dismounted and after hurriedly removing the muffles from their saddle rolls, coaxed their horses to suffer them. When they moved out of the valley they moved along the rock floor of the exit as silently as ghosts.

The route twisted and turned its way

through the mountain, the hard rocky floor showing up the recent scratches and scores made by shod horses. Clint and Mex traversed the narrow passage at little more than walking pace, taking the usual precaution at each bend, and by the time they emerged on the eastern shoulder of the mountain, an hour had slipped away. They paused for a while, scanning the slopes and the plain far below for a sight of Dillon or Lear, but there was no trace and Mex brought his attention back to the deer trail that ringed the mountain. The recent hoofmarks were plain enough to see; Lear and Dillon had turned north along the face of the mountain.

'I reckon Lear's making the ride as hard as he can in the hope of Dillon's cayuse giving out,' remarked Clint. 'He knows durned well that Dillon near rode it into the ground catching up with him in the first place.'

Mex grinned and pointed to the north where the river spilled out of the mountain and started its wanderings over Bar Q and Triple Bar graze.

'They'll sure enough hit some rough country where that river comes from,' he said.

As they shaded their eyes to get a clearer view of what lay ahead they saw a rider far away, where the mountain bulged into view again after having rounded away to the west. Keeping the rider in sight, the pards slid out of their saddles and removed the muffles from their horses' hooves. By the time they had remounted, the second rider, who they knew to be Dillon, had cleared the cover of the mountain's shoulder.

'Lear's keeping just outa rifle range,' Mex grunted. 'It's my guess he's leading Dillon on like a bull ringed at the nose.'

Clint rubbed his homely face free of sweat and taking a sparing drink of water out of his canteen, offered it to Mex.

'Well, let's get after 'em,' he said as the Mexican allowed the liquid to trickle slowly down his throat. 'After following the bustards this far I sure do want to see how they sort 'emselves out.'

Mex led the way and Clint followed as soon as he had replaced his canteen. They did not push their mounts but both horses still had a lot of reserve strength left and they travelled at a steady mile-eating pace with the sure-footed aplomb of the mountain deer who had originally carved the trail.

The route led up to the rim of the mountain as it veered away to the west, and down to the shoulder again when it curved back to the point where the pards had seen Lear and Dillon. They were now making faster progress than their quarry and both men felt a mounting curiosity as they tried to visualize what the end of the trail would bring. They rounded a vast hump of the mountain to a point that opened up another wide stretch of the contours ahead. About a mile away was the gouged channel that the river had carved down the mountain side, and the sun glinted on its ribbon-like surface in the plain. There was a horseman making a scrambling climb up the lip of the gorge but the distance was too great for the pards to decide whether it was Dillon or Lear.

Their doubts were resolved almost at once. They saw a minute puff of smoke further down the rim of the gorge, seconds before the rifle shot echoed around them, and they saw the animal check its scrambling run when almost at the head of the gorge. A figure detached itself from the fallen animal after a minute's pause and ran a zig-zag course to the cover of a boulder. They saw Dillon emerge from cover and move slowly up near the edge of the gorge. He darted for cover when a shot sent its thunder reverberating around the mountain slopes. Clint and Mex exchanged glances. That was a rifle shot so Lear must have been carrying a rifle in his saddle roll. This could turn into a long drawn-out battle.

Mex pointed to a spot alongside the gorge some distance below Dillon, and traced a route across the mountain side where they could travel with very little chance of being spotted. Clint followed his companion's moving finger intently and agreed they should try their luck.

The rifles were barking every few seconds, each shot building up into a noise like a roll of thunder as it echoed and bounced from surface to surface. The pards made their careful way to their objective, all the time using the terrain to mask their passage. They made the shelter of a steep shelf about three hundred yards below the point where Dillon crouched behind a couple of boulders about fifty yards away from the edge of the gorge.

The pards were about to slide out of their saddles when they both spotted something that immediately held their attention. Just a few yards away from them and about forty yards away from the edge of the gorge was a crack in the ground about nine inches wide. They traced its passage down the slope for two hundred yards. How far up the mountain side it ran they could only guess. Any attempt to find out for themselves would take with it the risk of exposing themselves to Lear's fire.

As they watched, dust and dirt dribbled along the line of the crack disappearing into its depths. At each rifle shot the fissure seemed to shudder and widen. Their mounts shied and backed nervously. Clint and Mex tried to calm them but both animals became almost unmanageable in their frenzy to get away.

Two more rifle shots started the build-up of echoing thunder and presaged a tearing, grinding sound lower down the mountain, then the ground started to tremble under them. The pinto and dun gelding were up on their hind legs and the pards had a momentary view of the ground above them. The crack ran almost to the top of the mountain and Dillon was crouched behind his boulder between the crack and the lip of the gorge. The horses pirouetted around on their back legs and the pards, exchanging a rapid glance, loosened their hold on the animals, giving them their heads.

The ripping and tearing sound rose into a screaming crescendo and the whole mountain seemed to shake. As their horses raced away from the scene, Clint and Mex were slewed in their saddles watching the phenomenon with wide eyes. Dust spewed up from the gorge in clouds that spiralled up into the blue heavens, blotting out the sky. They watched in awe as the whole lip of the gorge from the crack to the edge slid away out of sight to accompanying thunder as a few million tons of mountain piled up in the gorge. They hauled their mounts to a prancing stop and stared back at the scene of the avalanche. The rumbling still rolled on as the new cliff face cleared itself of loosened boulders, and the dust clouds rose like a pall over the mountain. They saw Lear briefly, standing staring at the new chasm that had opened up just a few feet away from him, then the dust blocked him out: but of Dillon there was no sign. He had gone with the avalanche. His horse was running fast across the face of the mountain back the way it had come, preservation proving too strong for the habit of remaining ground hitched.

With the danger passed their own mounts calmed down but when Clint and Mex slid to the ground, their horses were still trembling in every limb.

'Phew!' Clint mopped his streaming face and stared back at the gorge. 'I guess Nugent's got a mighty strong sidekick somewhere but it sure took a powerful lot of noise to put paid to Dillon.'

Mex nodded, his eyes glued on the place where Lear had vanished behind the dust. 'Yeah, and that leaves just one. Don Lear. When he gets over the shock of what's happened, he'll be thinking he's in the clear. I'm durned sure he had no eyes for us with the mountain opening up at his feet.'

After leading their horses to a shallow fold, where they would be out of Lear's view, the pards stretched at full length and waited for the dust to clear. The rumbling and crashing went on in a desultory manner and would no doubt carry on for some days until just the smooth cliff face remained, but the dust was lessening each minute. At last Lear emerged, the last dust particles swirling around him and on up into the blackened sky.

He gave one last look at the chasm, rubbed the dirt out of his eyes, and bending down behind the boulder that had sheltered him, he reappeared with the saddle-bags he must have removed from his dead horse. Lear heaved them over his shoulder and picked up his rifle. He paused a moment in thought, and making his decision threw the rifle back down, then started on down the hill. Clint and Mex exchanged grins.

The Bar Q segundo was covered in alkali from head to foot but his eyes gleamed bright with victory. The money he carried in the saddle-bags was now his. There was no one left with whom to share. The way he saw things he could return to the Bar Q in the course of time and take over where Dillon had left off, but with money enough for his needs he doubted whether he would take up that option. He was close to where the pards lay in wait, walking stiff-legged in his high heeled boots. He stiffened and stood wooden-faced when Mex yelled.

'Freeze, Lear!'

Mex was kneeling now, a gun held steady as a rock in his right hand and Clint hauled himself to his feet, both guns out. Lear stood transfixed, unable to grasp that the game was played out. He made two or three attempts to frame words before finally finding voice.

'What're you hombres doin' on Bar Q range?' he managed at last. 'You'd better pack the hardware an' get movin'.'

'Cut the innocent act, Lear,' Clint growled. 'We've been on your tail all day, night too for that matter, starting with what Nugent saw you taking out of Dillon's safe. We saw you turn the herd back on Dillon's outfit and we were right below Dillon when you were slinging lead at each other.'

Lear said nothing but he was watchful and mean-looking.

'Drop those saddle-bags and unhitch your gunbelt.' The Mexican's voice was brittle.

Lear shook his head decisively. 'I don't reckon you hombres would shoot a man in the back,' he said. 'An' I aim to go on walking down this hillside.'

Mex laughed but without mirth. 'You're plumb right Lear, but you're as much a man as a long-tailed skunk. I'd plug your back as free as I'd fill your belly with lead. Now, if you've got a fancy for living until the necktie party gets you, drop your guns and those saddle-bags.'

Lear's face worked and his eyes spat hate as he weighed the possibilities, then he gave what appeared to be a resigned shrug before slowly reaching for the connecting strap to the saddle-bags. In a split second he galvanized into action. Hurling the saddle-bags at the pards, he ran past them like a man demented. As Clint and Mex dodged the heavy leather satchels and struggled with each other to clear the encumbrance, Lear reached the horses. He kept Bellamy's dun gelding between him and the pards as he sent it running, riding Apache fashion. Mex leaped down to his pinto's side and within seconds was hot on the man's trail. Clint glared down at the saddle-bags in disgust and after watching the two riders until they disappeared from view, walked towards the edge of the gorge, curious to see what all the noise had been about.

Throughout the years the river must have gouged a deep channel through the mountain side but the fallen length of cliff face had now nullified the work of centuries. The river channel was almost filled with rocks and debris as far as Clint could see. Still curious, the Texan ran scrambling up the mountain. He wanted to know what was happening to the water that previously had run freely down the gorge on to the Bar Q. He was not particularly worried about Mex. Lear was fast and as dangerous as a mountain lion but the Mexican would take no chances.

Clint reached the top and gazed over the pile of debris to the natural river channel beyond. He fixed his gaze on a jutting slab of limestone just above water level and watched the water rise slowly to cover it. The river would have to rise another fifty feet before it could swill over the dam caused by the landslide. He looked back along the course of the river through the mountains, and as far as he could see the fall towards the dam was so slight as to be non-existent.

Lear had gained enough ground initially to swing up into the saddle and ride normally. He reasoned that riding at speed over this coarse ground would make him a difficult target and he settled down to the race calmly. He thought savagely that he was far from finished yet. Once he'd dealt with the greaser, then Bellamy, being on foot, would be easy meat. He would still end up with the dinero.

Unknown to Lear, Mex was dictating the speed. Normally there was little to choose between the pinto and Bellamy's gelding but the pinto had the edge on sleep and Mex knew he could run Lear down when he wished. A savage grin split Juarez' mouth as a thought struck him and he searched the terrain ahead to obtain the maximum aid.

Lear kept darting quick looks over his shoulder, and a couple of times sent bullets whining well wide of his pursuer. When the side of the mountain fell away more steeply a few hundred yards ahead, Mex let the pinto stretch, narrowing the gap rapidly. He rode low over his mount's neck, presenting no target, but watching Lear for the inevit-

227

able mistake.

The Bar Q segundo cast another quick look and the racing animals were close enough now for Mex to catch the expression on his face. Lear jammed his spurs deep into the gelding's flanks and flew over the outraged animal's head when the horse screamed in displeasure and came to an abrupt, bucking, kicking stop. Lear hit the ground hard and rolled about fifty feet down the mountainside before his body came against the solid bulk of a protruding boulder. Mex had halted his pinto and was standing clear of the animals, waiting for Lear to pull himself together.

Slowly Lear hauled himself on to his knees. He shook his head a few times then regained his feet and raised his glance to meet the Mexican's. He found little comfort there. The Mexican's eyes glittered like coals of fire in a cave and his mouth was a cruel hard line.

'You can take your choice, Lear,' Mex gritted at length. 'You can draw or I'll gun you down cold. I'm taking you in dead anyway.'

Lear, callous to the last degree, had no reason to doubt the Mexican's intention and with the die cast his gunman instincts came quickly to his aid. His face became masklike and he allowed the tension to drain away from him as he gauged the Mexican's ability. Such was his ego that he still considered his chances were sixty-forty.

No more than half a minute went by before the guns erupted, but to both men it was a lifetime. Their eyes were closed to all but their opponent in front, their ears rejecting the life that went on around them. Mex waited for Lear to make his move. He had a grim purpose in giving the man first chance.

The moment came and Lear went like lightning for his gun. As it cleared leather, the Mexican's guns belched flame and Lear stood staring at his hands incredulously. The gun dropped from his nerveless hands and the blood reached the end of his fingers and dripped to the ground. He brought his gaze up slowly to the Mexican and black hatred bridged the gap between them.

'If you don't get a necktie party, Mister, you'll have to learn to live honestly. You're never gonna be any great shakes with the hardware again.' Mex paused. 'Not that you stacked up to much before,' he added. 'Bellamy now, he's a shade faster'n me, and way back in Montana there's a coupla hombres that make Bellamy look like he's sleeping.'

His remarks were calculated and he drew satisfaction at the way Lear's shoulders sagged. The blood dripped steadily down from Lear's hand and the man stared back at him, completely bemused. Mex brought him back to reality by firing a bullet within an inch of his feet.

'Get back in the saddle Lear or I'll put a slug in each leg,' he growled.

Lear moved up the slope like an automaton and after a dozen unsuccessful attempts to get back into the saddle, finally made it. Mex watched him, unmoved.

'Now get going back to where we left Bellamy. Any attempt to run for it and I plug you where it'll hurt.'

The feeling had started to return to Lear's shattered hands, bringing pain in ever increasing tempo and ease was of greater concern to him than escape. By the time they arrived back to where Lear had made his break the man was slumped in the saddle.

Clint was at the top of the mountain waving Mex on up, so he urged Lear up in front of him. They drew alongside Clint who took in Lear's condition at a glance, and Mex followed Bellamy's pointing finger.

The water that had built up behind the dam was now running back along its course. The river had found another outlet down to the plain. An understanding look passed between the pards. At last they knew why Dillon had wanted the Triple Bar so badly. A long time later when they rode past the point where the river almost touched the mountainside on the Triple Bar, after its long curving course through Bar Q range, water was running with ever increasing volume down a long gulley, cascading the last few feet into its own bed on the plains. In time it would wear away all opposition and the bed now drying up on the Bar Q would fill with dust, leaving little trace of its existence.

It was past sundown when they rode into Twin Springs. The pards had shared the chore of bringing Lear in, taking it in turns to ride double, and were now heartily glad to be rid of his unwelcome company. Lear was too far gone from loss of blood and pain to notice what was happening when they ushered him into the gaol-house. When Clint directed him into a cell he dropped on to the bunk and held up his roughly bandaged hands.

'What're you gonna do about these?' he asked.

Clint took his time replying.

'I guess that depends on you,' he said easily. 'We already know what happened here the day of the bank steal after Cawson cleared the town with the tale of gold in Seminoe Peak.' He paused while Mex came alongside. 'But we just want to hear it again from you. Any lies and you'll rot where you sit, and there'll be no medical attention for those hands of yours.'

Lear's pain-filled eyes glassed a little, then he shrugged and pulled himself together.

'Reckon I've killed plenty in my time,' he said. 'But I had no hand in the killing of Rushland an' Cressy. Dillon brought the boys in on that job. He was that set on squeezing

231

Nugent off the Triple Bar before the mountain stove in an' cut off the water that killing old man Rushland and his sidekick didn't add up to much.'

'That split in the mountain's been opening up for some time then?' Mex put in.

Lear nodded. 'Yeah. 'Bout three years ago the first signs showed an' it wasn't long before Dillon got to thinking he'd have to take over the Triple Bar. Anyways, to get back to the bank steal, that day I was in Rawlins, laying it around I was waiting for Dillon, an' straight after the steal Dillon headed for Rawlins. He figured none of the townsfolk would have got back from Seminoe Peak so he planned to be aboard the stage from Rawlins and right alongside old Rube, the driver, when he delivered the usual package to the bank. It didn't quite work out that way. You hombres horned in.'

'All right Lear. I guess that ties things up. We'll see the doc gets here mighty soon and if you'll say your piece again in front of him, then for my money you can hightail it outa the territory,' Clint said before following Mex outside and locking the cell door.

Locking the gaol-house door was a mere formality. The window frame remained shattered as Dillon had left it, but with the inner door to the cell block locked, Lear was safe enough. They made their way to Seth Harben's hotel and found Harben in his tiny office. He bounced out of his chair in excitement as Clint and Mex entered.

'I'm plumb glad to see you fellers,' he said as he searched around for glasses and a bottle. 'I've been over to see Nugent at the Rushland's and got wised up on a few things.'

Both men grinned at his excitement, and sitting on the edge of his table, they took the glasses of bourbon he offered thankfully. Harben passed over a box of cheroots that made the Mexican's eyes glint. Clint shook his head and searched for his tobacco sack.

'Grab yourself a handful, Juarez,' Harben prompted, noting the appreciation on Mex's face as he lit up. Mex did so readily enough and grinned as Clint groaned and moved away.

Between them the pards told Harben the whole story and the hotel keeper remained silent throughout, completely enthralled. The only time he moved was to refill the glasses.

'By Jiminy!' he ejaculated finally. 'I reckon Twin Springs an' Nugent sure owe you fellers a piece for sorting this lot out. You gonna stay around?'

'We'll mebbe tidy things up a bit,' replied Clint. 'Then I guess we'll be riding on.' He paused while a disappointed look fleeted over Harben's face. 'But there's a couple things we want you to do right now.'

'You name 'em.' Harben was busy with the

bottle again.

Clint tossed the gaol-house key across the table.

'I guess you can harangue the townsfolk into electing a deputy until you can vote in a marshal.' Harben nodded. 'Well, get 'em together right away. We want Lear taken care of but we're done with wet nursing. And then we'd like you to raise about ten square-shooters for the Triple Bar. Have 'em ready for the trail by sun-up tomorrow and we'll pull those steers back outa the hidden valley.'

'Leave it to me,' the hotel man said. 'I guess you'll be wanting to see Nugent.'

Setting their glasses down, the pards nodded and pushed out of the hotel leaving Harben to his chores. Before calling on Kathy Rushland, they rode their mounts into the livery stable and took time out to ensure the animals would spend a well-deserved respite. When they eventually knocked at the Rushland's door, Mex was carrying Lear's saddle-bags. The door swung open and Kathy stood a moment peering into the darkness. When she recognized them a wide smile of welcome lit up her face and she reached out her hands to them, drawing them into the house.

'Oh – I'm so glad to see you both safe and sound,' she said, utter sincerity in her voice. 'And Matt, I guess the sight of you will set him well on the way to recovery.'

Both men smiled with her and followed when she bid them go with her. She led the way to a big bedroom at the rear of the house and ushered them in to where Matt Nugent lay pale but alert.

Clint and Mex came alongside the bed, smiling encouragement.

'The medico patch you up all right?' asked Mex.

'Yeah, he sure did a good job.' Nugent's voice was weak but the pards were glad to notice his eyes held no trace of fever. 'He got the slug out and said there's no reason why I shouldn't be as good as new in a few weeks.'

Kathy Rushland stood at the end of the bed, her eyes riveted on the man she loved, then satisfied he could talk without tiring himself she indicated a couple of chairs for the pards and went out of the room, returning later with bottle and glasses. When she sat down after pouring out drinks, Mex handed the saddle-bags over to her.

'You'll find there all that was taken from the bank and mebbe a lot more that belonged to Dillon. I guess he's lost interest in money,' he said. 'Anyways he won't be spending any more.'

The girl opened the saddle-bags and held up some of the thick wads of bank notes for Nugent to see. He had no need to talk. His gratitude showed plainly in his eyes. The girl let the notes drop back into the saddle-bags and regarded Clint and Mex for a long time, her eyes glistening.

'Thank you.'

Just once she said it, her voice husky, but such was the intensity of feeling behind the words that the pards reckoned it had all been worth while. She looked down again and they rightly guessed the relief that was sweeping through her because Rushland's bank could honour its obligations again. When she looked up she was smiling.

'Tell us,' she said. 'Please tell us all about it.'

Once again the pards told their story, minimizing their own parts and playing down the wholesale slaughter, but neither the girl nor the man were deceived. They knew the game had been played out between warring factions totalling about thirty men, and these two had come back bringing in a prisoner and the money.

Clint and Mex stood up and shook Nugent's extended hand.

'Time we hit the hay,' Clint said. 'It's been a long day.'

'I sure hope you fellers are staying on,' Nugent said. 'You've earned yourselves Dillon's spread. We can dig drain channels to get the water back on the Bar Q.'

'Nope, we aim to get that rustled beef back

on your graze,' Mex replied. 'Dillon's herd will sure enough find their way over following the water, then we'll be moving on.' He looked at the girl slyly. 'One thing that's likely to hold us a bit is a wedding. On account Clint's the sentimental type,' he added with a grin.

'Then you'll be staying a month,' Kathy Rushland said quickly. 'That's just about the time it's going to take for Matt to get on his feet again.'

There was a big smile on Nugent's face and for a moment he was lost to everything but the happiness that was his. Kathy met his gaze and went to take his outstretched hands. Clint and Mex looked at each other, grinned delightedly, and tiptoed away. They were at the front door when Kathy Rushland caught up with them.

'You will stay for the wedding?' she asked, her big blue eyes pleading.

'Yes, we'll stay,' they replied in unison.

'We sure need you,' said Kathy. 'One of you will be best man and the other will have the job of giving me away.'

She stayed at the door for a while, listening to them arguing regarding the merits of the particular functions she had outlined for them and bickering good-naturedly over who should do what, then with a smile of contentment she shut the door quietly and went back upstairs to her man.